www.SaucyRoma

Marrying Her Rich Asian Widower

From grief to the love of a lifetime!

An emotional yet sexy romance by best selling BWAM author Mary Peart.

David is a recent widower, who was in an arranged marriage with a woman he didn't love. But respect is big in his culture.

So when he visits a florist to collect some flowers for his wife's grave, he's surprised to find the shop owner and himself seem to hit it off.

He reluctantly agrees to meet this woman Janice again, but feels guilty about having feelings for someone else when he wasn't a great husband to his first wife.

Janice, however, is smitten, and knows that David is the man she wants to be with. Will she be able to convince him she's the one he could spend his life with?

Or will his guilt be too much for both of them to bear?

Find out in this emotional yet steamy roller coaster of a romance by bestselling author Mary Peart.

Suitable for over 18s only due to sex scenes so hot, you'll be on the lookout for your own Asian billionaire to seduce.

Get Free Romance eBooks!

Hi there. As a special thank you for buying this book, for a limited time I want to send you some great ebooks completely **free of charge** directly to your email! You can get it by going to this page:

www.saucyromancebooks.com/physical

You can see a the cover of these books on the next page:

www.SaucyRomanceBooks.com/RomanceBooks

These ebooks are so exclusive you can't even buy them. When you download them I'll also send you updates when new books like this are available.

Again, that link is:

www.saucyromancebooks.com/physical

Copyright © 2016 to Mary Peart and SaucyRomanceBooks.com. No part of this book can be copied or distributed without written permission from the above copyright holders.

www.SaucyRomanceBooks.com/RomanceBooks

Contents

Chapter 1

“Mom, I cannot discuss that with you right now. I have several deliveries to make and the van has been giving me hell since yesterday.” Janice rummaged through her closet to find something suitable to wear to work. Nothing in her closet looked even remotely like something she wanted to wear. She was supposed to go shopping with her two best friends Leah and Candace, but that had not happened yet.

“You are breaking your mother’s heart, honey,” Janet complained.

“Mom, what do you care that Dad is getting married to some bimbo? I thought you were over him ages ago.”

“I am sweetie, it is just the principle of the thing. He is getting married to the bimbo just to spite me.”

“I strongly doubt that.” She pulled out a long floral dress and gave it a frowning look. It will have to do. She could team it with a white jacket. It was spring and the weather was a little on the cold side. “You have been dating since you and Dad have been divorced and that has been over five years now.”

“Yes honey, but you are providing flowers to the competition.”

“I am providing flowers to a paying customer and I have no problem doing that,” Janice corrected her. She was tired of being caught in the middle of her parents’ ongoing arguments and drama, and she wished they would keep her out of it.

“I saw them the other day at the supermarket and she was clinging to his arms like a love-struck kitten, it made me sick to look at them.”

“Mom, you need to move on and I thought you had. You keep telling me that, but it seems to me that you are still hanging on to something that has been dead for years.” Janice stared at herself in the mirror critically. She looked more like her father than her mother. She had gotten his amazing dark brown eyes and his mouth, but she had inherited her mother’s strong black curls that framed her oval face beautifully. Her mouth was all her own, full and generous and needed no artifice.

“We were married for twenty years honey, which has to count for something. I am surprised you are taking it so well,” her mother complained.

“You guys were very unhappy long before the divorce and I noticed that. So I think the best thing to do is be apart. If it does not work, then it’s time to let go,” Janice said practically. “Tell you what, I will be around there this weekend and you can bitch about Dad the entire time. How about that?”

“Okay, talk to you later,” she said with a sniff. “I think I hear Maud calling from next door. Bye honey.”

Her parents had separated five years ago when she was still in college doing her horticultural degree, but she had seen it coming. Each weekend, she had come home to find that the silences between them were getting more and more, and although they had tried to keep it together when she was there, it was very apparent. Her mother had accused her father of cheating on her and he had accused her of being cold and distant. So they had parted and he had left the house to her and gone to live in an apartment. He had called her a month ago and told her he had met someone and was planning on getting married. “Have you told Mom?” she had asked him.

“I was thinking you would,” he told her with a laugh.

"Are you serious, Dad?" she had asked him in exasperation. "You and Mom need to sort this thing out between you."

"You know how crazy your mother gets, sweetie. As soon as we start talking, she starts arguing and I cannot deal with that," he protested. She had never held any resentment towards him because he was a very good father and always treated her with love and respect. They had a standing lunch engagement every Thursday afternoon, and no matter what happened, he always made it.

"Tell her, Dad," she said firmly. "I am not going there." She paused. "Do you love her?"

"Your mom?"

"No, the woman you are getting married to."

"I love your mother, sweetie, but we grew apart years ago and we could never seem to get it back. Charlene is a sweet girl and I know you probably think she is a bit on the young side, but I care about her very much and I don't like to be by myself for too long," he told her wryly.

"Tell Mom please, and don't allow her to hear it from someone else," she had advised him.

*****

"We have an order for some tulips, jasmine, and muscari, and Mrs. Hanover ordered some dogwood trees for her garden," Maggie said as soon as she came into the store. The smell of the different flowers and trees hit her as soon as she entered and she went immediately to put away some small bulbs she had picked up on her way the store. It was eight-thirty and the beautiful spring morning had delayed her journey to the store as she had stopped to listen to the birds chirping and looked at the amazing array of flowers along the road. Spring was her favorite time of the year, and she always thought it brought a feeling of hope along with it.

"What about the order for Mr. Jenkins?" She sniffed a sprig of rosemary on her way around the greenhouse, stopping to put away her pocketbook and her spring jacket.

"Jake already took it." Maggie passed her a latte she had brought on her way to work. "We have the wedding bouquets to deal with for Saturday and the bride called and said she is going to need additional jasmines and dahlias for the decoration."

"Do I have time to finish my coffee?" she asked the woman teasingly, sipping the latte appreciatively.

"Barely," Maggie told her with a smile, going off as she heard the front door bell chime. "We also need to discuss the arrangements for the spring festival," she called out.

She had always known that she was going to be working with plants. When she was just a little girl, she had asked her parents for spades and buckets and had started digging in the dirt and planting things, making sure to water them and had watched them grow. The love for plants had not waned when she grew up but had heightened, and when she was in high school, she had already had her own backyard with fruits vegetables and flowers so it was natural for her to continue and she had never regretted it.

She had opened Beautiful Bouquets two years now and she was doing exceptionally well. The phone rang just then and she knew her day had started.

*****

David Hattori stared at the list of vehicles that had been shipped off from Japan. He had placed orders for high-end vehicles and there had been a little delay in his getting them in the country, but they were here now and orders had already been made to get them off his hands. Hattori Vehicle Imports and Exports was one of the most lucrative and successful business in the country and it had started with his grandfather, a native of Japan, who had come over with his family some sixty years ago. His grandfather, Matthew Hattori, had started the business selling used cars until he had upgraded to brand-new vehicles. His son, David's father, who had been born here had taken over from him, had taken the business to the next level, turning it into a billion-dollar company. He had died of a heart attack a year ago and left the company to his son to carry on. His mother was still alive and spent her time doing pottery and decorating ceramics to fill her time.

There was a soft knock on his office door before it was pushed open. "You said I should remind you about the meeting in the conference room, David," his secretary told him. She was a middle-aged Japanese woman who had been first with his father and now him.

“Thanks, Julia,” he murmured with a brief nod. He had been staring at the calendar and knew the dreaded day was coming up and he was not looking forward to it.

*****

“How about marigolds, Mrs. Robinson? Janice asked the elderly lady as she wandered around the store and looked at the various plants there. The woman had been a regular for the past year and she loved flowers and she was also one of her best customers.

“I was thinking of trying Camellia or Snowdrop or even the pansies,” she murmured. She had lost her husband three years ago and was childless so she spent her time puttering in her garden and doing charitable work around the neighborhood.

“I think those are good choices.” Janice hurried over look for the requested plants and talked her through the caring of them.

“I might as well pick up some lilacs and peonies as well,” Mrs. Robinson told her. “Did I tell you I was having the members of the gardening club over this Saturday?" she asked, her watery blue eyes lighting up with a smile.

"You did not!" Janice said enthusiastically. "I wish I could be there, but I have a wedding this Saturday."

"Your expertise could come in handy," Mrs. Robinson said in regret.

"Next time perhaps."

*****

Janice closed and locked the door behind her and pulled her dress over her head and went straight to the bathroom. She loved her plants, but for half the day she spent the time digging around her greenhouse and the smell of the plants and dirt usually clung to her. She set the tone for the bath, making sure there was music and poured some bath salts into the warm sudsy water. Pulling off her underwear, she sank into the water with a contented sigh. Her work hours were long, but she enjoyed it, but sometimes the hassle of the delivery was too much for the day and she had had to take the van to the mechanic for him to have a quick look at it. He had told her she needed a new alternator.

She soaked for an hour and then got out when the water was cooling and went to the kitchen to heat up some leftover soup.

Her phone rang just as she was about to wash out the bowl.

“Dad, hi,” she answered seeing his name come up.

“How is my favorite daughter?” he asked in his deep reassuring voice.

“Your only daughter,“ she reminded him dryly. “What’s going on?”

“Heard from your mother lately?” he asked her casually.

“I hear from Mom every day dad and you know that. What’s going on?” she asked suspiciously.

“She called me earlier and told me she wanted to see me urgently. Any idea what’s that about?”

“No idea whatsoever. Why didn’t you ask her on the phone?”

“She said she was not going to discuss anything of importance over the phone with me,” he said “I thought maybe she would have given you a hint as to what she had to discuss.”

"Not one." She paused. "Does what's her name know you communicate with Mom almost every day?"

"Her name is Charlene, honey, and you already know that," her father said dryly. "She knows that I have been with your mother for so many years and we still have a connection. She understands."

"She must be quite a woman," Janice said with a laugh. "Are you okay, Dad?"

"Yes I am baby girl, thanks for asking and thanks for not making a big deal about me marrying another woman," he said appreciatively.

"I am a grown woman now, Dad, and would rather you and Mom parted than to be miserable together," she said honestly.

"Thanks hon," he said warmly. "See you on Thursday?"

"Absolutely," she responded. "Your time to pick up the tab," she reminded him.

"Of course," he said with a laugh. "Love you girl."

"Love you too, Dad."

*****

“That looks lovely.” Julie Hattori looked up as she heard her son’s voice in the doorway. She had been so caught up in painting the symbols on the cups that she had lost all track of time.

“David, I did not hear you come in,” she exclaimed, wiping her hands on the apron she put on over her clothes to keep it from getting messed up. She was an exquisitely beautiful woman, and her son took most of his looks from her with the same fine dark hair and haunted look on his chiseled face. David Hattori did not smile much and when he did, it was such a transformation that it was like a whole new person. He had taken the strong jaw and height from his father and the regal bearing from his mother.

“You were so caught up in your work that you would not have heard a bomb drop,” he told her with a whimsical smile, coming into the room. It was a room she had made hers with large glass windows that let in the light from all angles and her work station set up to do her designs. There was even a mini-fridge in the corner loaded with cold cuts and fruits and different beverages.

“How was work?” She took off the apron and folded it over a chair, revealing the mint green kimono she was wearing.

“The vehicles came in today,” he told her briefly. He sat on one of the couches and looked around the room as if he was searching for something. “It was a good day.”

Julie sat beside him, not touching him but letting him feel her presence. Her son was grieving and was barely living and her heart ached for him. It would have been a little acceptable if he had been in love with her, but it had been an arranged marriage between two families and he had never loved her, but she had fallen in love with him and from the accident a year ago, he had been carrying the guilt with him.

“Will you be going in next week?” she asked him softly, knowing what he was thinking.

“It makes me feel better to work, Mother.” He stared off into space. He remembered her telling him that she had wanted a child and he had told her that to bring a child into a loveless marriage would be a mistake. She had died the week after on her way home from work. It had been a pile-up and she had been one of the fatalities. He never loved her and he always let her knew that. He had moved from the apartment they had been living in and came back home. His father had died a month after that.

“How about we go somewhere next weekend?” she asked him softly.

“We will see,” he told her with a fond smile. “I need to get some paperwork done so I will see you at dinner.”

Julie watched him leave the room with sad eyes and wished she could take away his pain. He had not wanted to marry her, but the families had thought it was a very good match and had persuaded him. Besides, Eileen Fujimoto had been in love with him since they had been a teenager and was never afraid to show it, the poor thing had thought that marrying David would have made him fall in love with her, but it had never happened.

With a sigh, Julie stood up and took up a photo of her late husband that was always on her desk. She had not been in love with when they got married but had grown to love him as the years went by. They had thought the same thing would have happened to their son and Eileen.

*****

“How about this one?” Leah held up a soft blue dress with a flowing skirt for Janice to look at. They were in the mall after both she and Candace had dragged her from the store late Friday afternoon to go shopping.

“There is a sale going on and we need clothes,” Candace had told her firmly.

So now they were in the mall.

“I don’t have the breasts to carry off that neckline,” Janice said decisively.

“Of course you do!” Leah looked at her bosom critically. She was a nurse at the local hospital and was currently going through a divorce. She had started the proceedings last month after a trial separation that had not worked out. “Go and try it on.”

She did and was surprised that it actually suited her. They picked up a few more items to add to the pile that was already there before going to the cashier.

“I think I am attracted to Jeremy,” Candace said as soon as they were out of the store. She worked as an executive secretary at a shipping company and Jeremy was her immediate boss.

“That’s a really bad idea, Candace,” Leah told her grimly. They had stopped at the pizza place inside the mall and had ordered pepperoni and Coke. “Look what happened to Lance and me.” Her estranged husband was a fellow nurse at the hospital she worked.

“That doesn’t mean it is going to happen to us,” Candace protested. She was tall and slender because she was always dieting and wore her shoulder-length hair in a chic bun at the nape of her neck. Leah, on the other hand, was petite and curvy with a short bob that brushed against her cheeks whenever she moved. “Anyway, the matter is moot considering that he does not even notice that I am a woman.”

“Consider yourself lucky,” Leah said, biting into her pizza with relish.

“In the meantime, Dad and Mom are at it again,” Janice told them with a grimace. She told them about the conversation she had had first with her mother and then with her dad.

"I bet those two are going to get back together eventually," Leah predicted with a grin.

"Lord help us," Janice said.

*****

Janet opened the door to let him in. She had just come in from the accounting office where she worked and had taken a shower and put on a loose cotton dress and had poured herself a glass of wine. Her heartbeat quickened as she looked at him standing there framed in the doorway, his dark brown eyes smiling at her. He was a very handsome man and she had always known that, no wonder he was irresistible to the opposite sex.

"Come on in." She moved aside to let him pass. "I am surprised the bim- the fiancé is not with you."

Richard looked at her wryly. "You were about to say bimbo, weren't you?"

"Absolutely not." She brushed past him to get him a glass to pour his wine. "I would never say something like that."

“You are something else, aren’t you?” Richard took the wine from her and went into the cozy living room of the home he had lived in before he left five years ago. She had not changed a thing. “What did you want to talk to me about?”

“I want to sell the house,” she told him, sipping her wine and looking at him thoughtfully.

“Why?” he asked with a frown.

“Because I am alone in a four-bedroom house. You have moved on and have another life and our daughter hardly ever come around.” She placed her half-empty glass on the coffee table.

“I thought you loved the neighborhood,” he said.

“I do, but I am lonely here, Richard, and I don’t see the sense of hanging on to a house that hold so many memories of us,” she explained.

“What do you want me to say, Jan?” he asked her, leaning forward to look at her. She had always been a beautiful woman, and with age she had mellowed with only slight creases around her dark brown eyes. He found himself regretting that they were no longer married.

“I want your advice and I want your help in looking for a smaller place,” she told him.

“I am sorry,” he said suddenly.

“What for?” she asked him puzzled.

“For us not working out,” he told her softly.

He stood up and so did she and without any warning at all they reached for each other, their lips meeting.

Janet felt the stir of desire trickle through her and with a sigh she returned the kiss, her arms going around his neck. Whatever else had been wrong in their marriage, the sex had always been very good and it was no different now!

Chapter 2

“Someone looks very lost,” Maggie whispered in an undertone. It had rained in the early morning and the smell of the rain on the flowers was very refreshing. The wedding had gone on well and the bride had thanked her effusively for the lovely arrangements.

Janice looked up from the floral arrangement she was doing and saw him. He was of Asian descent and was tall and sober looking in an obviously expensive charcoal grey suit. He was looking at the various flowers displayed.

She left what she was doing and walked over to where he was. He did not seem to notice that she had come up beside until she spoke. “What are you looking for?” she asked him softly.

He turned to look at her and she saw his eyes drifting over her face coolly before he responded. “I am looking for something to put on my wife’s grave.”

“Oh, I am so sorry,” she exclaimed. No wonder he looked so sad and distant. He was tall and dark and his black hair was combed severely back from a broad forehead and he had the most intense black eyes she had ever seen. “How long?”

“A year today.” He turned back to the array of flowers. “I am afraid I don’t know what to choose.”

“What was her favorite kind?”

He turned back to look at her and his confusion was apparent. What sort of husband did not know his wife’s favorite flowers?

“I like tulips myself and snowdrop anemone,” she told him conversationally, pointing to the plants. “Or maybe pansies.”

“How about I get all of them?” he asked, giving her a grateful look.

“Good choice,” she told him cheerfully, going around selecting his order. She packaged the plants carefully and put some sprigs of rosemary there as well. He handed her a platinum card to pay for his purchase and she rang up the sale. She wished she could talk to him some more and find out what happened and if children were involved, but he was clearly not the divulging of information type.

She held out a hand as he was about to leave. “My name is Janice and thank you for shopping here.”

He hesitated briefly, looking at her slender elegant hand and then he took it in his with a nod. “David Hattori.”

Her eyes widened as he released her hand. “You are the high-end vehicles Hattori,” she exclaimed.

“I am afraid so.” A tiny smile actually lifted his mouth. He was quite a handsome man, she thought suddenly, but his face was etched in sadness that took away from it.

“I love your ads on television, but I am afraid I cannot afford even the tires on one of those vehicles,” she told him with a smile. He was caught by it and he stood there staring at her for a moment before he looked away. Janice’s smile was like a magnet and lit up her entire face as if there was a particularly bright light shining from within her. She had beautiful white teeth with a tiny gap in the front and she had dimples on both cheeks.

“Thank you,” he muttered and hurried away.

Janice stood there staring after him wondering if she had said something wrong.

“Someone certainly looked skittish,” Maggie commented, looking at the man’s departing back.

“Today is a year since his wife died,” Janice commented automatically.

“Oh dear Lord.” Maggie shook her head sadly. “No wonder he looks like that, the poor guy.”

“Ever heard about Hattori’s Vehicles Import and Export?” Janice asked her.

“Who hasn’t?”

“That’s David Hattori,” she said with a nod.

“You are kidding me!” Maggie’s large dark brown eyes went round in her round face. “He actually came in to buy the flowers himself? He must have really loved that wife of his!”

*****

David placed the flowers against the headstone that read: 'Gone too soon' – Eileen Hattori: Born: July 16, 1991. Died: April 10, 2015. He stood there looking at the cold grey stone, a frown etched on his brow. He had been punishing himself since she died and had not gone out with anyone since. He felt he owed her that much for not loving her when he should have. The flowers added a splash of color to the lifeless grave and his heart constricted for a life so young that had gone too soon. His mother had offered to come with him, but he wanted to do it by himself. Her parents had gone back to live in Japan soon after their daughter's death and had not kept in touch with him or his family. He understood perfectly. He was alive and their only child was dead, how could they relate to him?

His eyes were drawn to the floral arrangement and his mind flashed suddenly to the friendly girl that had chosen them for him. Her smile came to mind and he felt a stir of awareness for the first time since his wife's death. He took a deep breath and forcibly exorcised it from his mind. With a last look at the grave, he walked away.

*****

“Mom, you did not have to go through all this trouble. I would have been satisfied with just a sandwich,” Janice protested as she came inside the kitchen and saw her mother taking out the pot roast. The smell permeated the air and there was also a lemon meringue pie cooling on the counter. There was a big bowl of salad on the counter as well and there were also mashed potatoes. Janet Langley was an attractive woman who was a legal secretary in a large law firm. She had been studying to do law when she got pregnant with Janet and decided to give it up. She had come from work an hour ago and had started to cook in anticipation of her daughter’s visit.

“Nonsense, girl.” She came over and gave her a swift kiss on one smooth cheek, her eyes taking in the red–and-white cotton dress she was wearing and the knee-length boots. Her daughter had her own unique sense of style and refused to wear any color that did not stand out. “When do I get the chance to go all out with my culinary skills? Grab some plates and let’s go into the dining room.”

“So how goes the floral business?” Janet asked as she sliced through the pot roast beef with the sharp knife.

She told her about David Hattori and how he had come in looking for flowers for his wife's grave.

"Poor man," Janet said shaking her head. "Life is so short and uncertain that's why we must take what we want from it and live it to the fullest."

Janet gave her a strange look as she put a heaping of mashed potatoes onto her plate. "Have you seen Dad?"

Her mother looked at her sharply, the knife she was using clattering to the edge of the plate. "What makes you ask that?"

"It's a simple question, Mom." Janice looked at her mother curiously, noticing that she was avoiding her eyes. "I spoke to him the other day and he said he was coming to see you."

"Ah yes, well he did." She busied herself sprinkling some salt onto her mashed potatoes.

"And?"

"And what?" Janet asked her impatiently. "Why all these questions?"

“Mom, what’s going on?” Janice put away her fork and gave her mother her full attention. She was behaving unlike herself.

“Can we talk about something else?” She dug into her salad. “It’s not like I have something to hide!”

“Oh Lord mom!” Janice exclaimed, staring at her mother in shock. “You slept with Dad, didn’t you?”

“Don’t be ridiculous! And what if I did? We were married for twenty-something years so nothing is wrong with that.”

“Mom, I thought you did not want to have anything to do with him?” Janice had to stop herself from laughing. What a mess! “You do realize that he is planning on getting married don’t you?”

“So?” she said defiantly. “He is not married yet is he? And it just happened. Don’t worry, it is certainly not going to happen again!”

*****

He came over that very night after calling her and telling her he was on his way. She opened the door to let him in and he took her into his arms. Now that he was with another woman, the attraction for him had certainly increased, she thought as they hurriedly undressed and got into bed, reaching for each other eagerly, their desire burning.

“I told our daughter this would never happen again,” she told him breathlessly as he slid out of her, his breathing ragged.

“You told her?” Richard’s voice sounded strangled.

“She came by for dinner and it just sort of popped out of my mouth,” she told him sheepishly. She wondered what he told her when he was with her, it would be interesting to hear.

“Janet,” he said with a groan.

“What?” she said carelessly. “It’s not like we are complete strangers.” With a coy smile she reached for his semi-erect penis and started squeezing it gently. “How about another round?”

“I have to go,” he muttered, feeling himself hardening again.

“Not just yet,” she told him firmly and pulled him close to her.

*****

“You should have seen the look on her face, guys, when I asked her about it.” Janice stirred her hot chocolate as she told her friends that her parents had slept together. “I can’t believe at their age that they are still doing it.”

“Your parents are middle-aged, honey, not elderly decrepit people who need help in the sex department,” Leah said with a grin. “I say hats off to them.”

“Isn’t he engaged to be married?” Candace asked curiously, sipping her latte. They had met for a mid-afternoon brunch because Leah had done a double shift and was on her way home to get some much needed sleep before going back to work tonight.

“He is, the last time I checked.” Janice said with a shake of her head. “Those two are going to be the death of me.”

“Lance wants us to give our marriage another chance.” Leah said abruptly, causing the other girls to look at her. “I know, I know. We have done the trial thing and it did not work but I saw him with another nurse the other day and I wanted to tear her in two. What is that telling me?”

“That you are still thinking of him as your husband.” Janice told her.

“Well technically he is,” Leah said with a sigh. “We started arguing in one of the on call rooms and we ended up having the greatest sex we have ever had since we got married.’

“I am convinced it’s something going around,” Janice said looking at her friend with a shake of her head. “First my parents and now you and Lance. You guys need to make up your minds.”

“It’s not as simple as that,” Leah protested. “Wait until you get into a relationship with someone, you will see.”

“That’s why I intend to wait until I am absolutely in love with the person before I start anything,” Janice said firmly.

*****

“Darling, you are not eating,” Julie remonstrated gently as she watched her son pushed the chicken and broccoli around on his plate. She had wanted to go with him to Eileen’s grave but he had told her a firm no and she had respected his wish but instead of looking better, he looked worse. She wished he would get over his guilt and get on with his life. All he did was work and come home and mope, he did not have a life and that was breaking her heart.

“I am not really hungry, Mother.” He smiled at her briefly and pushed away his plate. “I am planning to increase the sales department in the company. We are expanding with sales and not enough sales people out there.” He often discussed business with her, letting her act as a kind of sounding board. “We are test driving the new Toyota and so far it is doing quite well. There was a scare for a little bit about the brakes not holding but that has been sorted out.”

“Thanks good,” Julie said with a nod, wishing he would not be so into the business. He had a lot on his plate being responsible for a billion-dollar company and the thousands of employees he had working for him. She wished his father was still alive to share some of the burdens. “I saw Arianna yesterday and she was asking about you,” she told him casually.

Arianna Blake was a beautiful Asian girl who had shown an interest in him six months ago when she had met him at the opening of the car mart downtown. She was a successful lawyer and had made her interest obvious but apart from being polite, David had not given her any encouragement.

“Mother, please don’t go there, I am not interested,” he told her firmly, making to leave the table. She knew what he was going to do. Go up to his very elegant suite and sit and stare broodingly out the balcony before going to bed.

“Okay darling,” she said hastily. “How about watching a movie with me? Your mother gets lonely sometimes.”

He looked at her quizzically and she had a feeling he was seeing right through her ruse, but with a brief nod he proceeded into the massive living room and used the remote to select a movie.

*****

He called and told her thanks for her very gracious help. She was pruning a dogwood tree around the greenhouse when her cell phone rang. It was Friday afternoon and the shop was not very busy so she had decided to do some work around the greenhouse. Deliveries had been sent out already for functions that were going to be happening over the weekend and Maggie was serving the one or two walk customers who came in. “Hello?” she answered uncertainly, not recognizing the number.

“Ms. Langley, this is David Hattori,” he told her, his deep voice stirring her blood. “I am just calling to tell you thanks for being so helpful the other day.”

“You re most welcome,” she told him, waiting for him to say something else.

“I was thinking of having you send some floral arrangements for a function we will be having here next weekend.” He paused as if he was consulting with someone. “It’s a luncheon for some out of town business associates of mine and I think it would be a welcome change to see some fresh flowers in the room.”

“I would be delighted to provide the floral arrangements,” she said, her heart pounding as she considered what it would mean to get business from such a big corporation. “I need to look at the décor of the room and decide what would suit best.”

“We do not open on Saturdays. Do you think you could come by tomorrow at around eleven?” he suggested. “I will be here and the guard downstairs will instruct you. Do you know where it is?"

"I do and I will be there. Thanks, see you then."

David put the phone on his desk. He had made the call on his cell phone because he had not wanted to go through the receptionists or his secretary. He had been thinking about her at odd times and had thought that maybe she would lively up the conference room. He had admired the way the floral displays had been set out in the store, it made the place look very inviting and the teal blue of the conference room could do with a little color. He forced himself not to think about her dazzling smile or the beautiful complexion because as far as he was concerned and nothing more!

*****

She arrived promptly at eleven and was told to go straight up. The building was quite impressive, mostly towering glass with the name of the company in big black letters. She had left Maggie at the store to deal with whatever it was and had driven over. She was told to take the private elevator straight to his office and she got off in a hallway where he met her. "Thank you for coming," he told her with a brief smile, unconsciously noticing how extremely good she looked in black denims and black silk blouse. Her hair was caught up in an untidy bun on top of her head and she was not wearing much make-up. “This way please.” He led her towards the long cylindrical conference room with its long table and chairs around it. There was an area where there was a small round table and she suspected that it was where refreshments were served. The view from the large and wide window was spectacular and showed a view of the landscape of the edge of the town with trees gently blowing in the breeze.

“What do you think?” She had been so deep in thought she had not heard him come up behind her as she stared outside.

She turned to look at the room and her mind quickly came up with a few ideas. “Some yellow and white roses for the center piece with a few begonias thrown in. We could put some calla lily and cornflower in the corners to bring some color to the place.”

“I like that.” He walked over to the window and stared outside, shoving his hands into the pockets of his faded blue denim pants. He was wearing a dark blue dress shirt and his hair was brushed back ruthlessly from his face. “I always love this view," he said absently and she had a feeling he was miles away. He turned to look at her. "Would you like to have some lunch?"

She looked at him in surprise.

"I have some things to go over and I suddenly do not feel the urge to do so yet," he told her with a faint smile. "I would be happy if you would join me for an early lunch."

She nodded, having a feeling that he did not want to be alone just now. "How about giving me a tour first?" she suggested.

He stared at her and then nodded leading the way out. The place was huge with offices showing different name tags and departments on each door. The entire décor was teal blue and the carpets a soft grey and she wondered what they had against bold colors. He took her downstairs to show her the show room with several brand new and expensive vehicles on display. She ran a hand over a shiny new red Toyota that would suit her fine, when she won the lottery.

"I would give you a good deal if you wanted it," he told her with a hint of amusement as he watched her.

“No thank you,” she said moving her hand away. “I would probably have to sell everything I own and even then I would still not be able to afford the payments.”

“If you change your mind…” he left the statement hanging and they went back up to his large and utilitarian office.

He saw the expression on her face and actually smiled. “I like simple surroundings. The chef leaves something here for me because he knows I come in on Saturdays and sometimes Sundays.” He told her, going into the fridge and taking out cold cuts to make sandwiches. “Please help yourself to whatever you want to drink.” He indicated a kind of juice bar and she poured herself some orange juice.

“What for you?”

“Some fruit punch, thanks.” He quickly whipped together two very large sandwiches and took them over to the table in the corner.

They were in the middle of eating when he spoke up. “I lost my wife a year ago and I am still in mourning,” he told her looking down at the sandwich he was eating.

“You must have loved her very much,” she told him sympathetically, wanting to reach out and touch him.

He looked at her considering for a moment then he put the sandwich down. “I would rather not discuss it if you don’t mind. I don’t know why I brought it up.”

“Okay no problem,” she told him easily. “Tell me about some of the things you do here.”

He told her about the company and the orders they had to fill on a daily basis.

“Don’t you ever feel overwhelmed?” she asked him in amazement.

“I love doing what I do,” he said with a faint smile. “What about you? Why plants?”

“I have a healthy fascination and I studied them in college. I love the smell and the different colors and am fascinated at the growth. I also love to play in the dirt.” She flashed that smile again and he found himself caught off guard like the first time. She was a stunningly beautiful woman!

Chapter 3

Charlene knew he was cheating on her. She just did not know who he was doing it with. He had not reached home until in the early hours of the morning because she had kept calling his home number and he had not picked up. She had also called his cell number, but it had been turned off. She had asked him to let her move in with him but he had refused saying he needed his solitude before they got married. What did she expect? He had cheated on his wife with her so she supposed it was payback.

Charlene Higgins was a tall attractive twenty-seven-year-old who had dated losers all her life until she met Richard Langley and he treated her with respect and kindness. She had fallen for him immediately and when he told her he was married she had not even cared because he was the best thing that had ever happened to her. When he had left his wife, she had been so secretly glad that she had gone and celebrated by herself. She had worked her way into his life so that he had started noticing her as more than just someone to give him a good time in bed. She had bid her time and finally he had asked her to marry him. It had been the happiest moment of her life. She was a small town girl with a high school education and who worked at a beauty salon and very soon she was going to be Mrs. Richard Langley and nothing or no one was going to stop her!

*****

Janice made the delivery herself. The function was going to be on Saturday and he had asked her if she mind doing the delivery on Friday after the staff had left for home. It would give her more time to set up. She had agreed promptly. He had asked for floral arrangements for his showroom as well as the reception area and Janice was very happy for the business. “I am hoping that this is a long term contract,” Maggie said enthusiastically as she helped to make the arrangements.

“I hope so too,” Janice said with a smile.

It was almost May, but the cold was lingering and a stiff breeze had come up today adding to the chill. It was a little past seven when she got to the office building and the same guard she had seen when she got there last week ushered her inside and told her to go straight up, Mr. Hattori was expecting her.

“I hope I am not keeping you from anything,” he said after he had greeted her politely and they made their way to the conference room.

“Not at all,” she told him immediately.

“I am surprised you are not going out on some date or the other,” he said, shocking both of them. “I am sorry, I have overstepped.”

“No,” she told him with a winning smile. “It’s quite okay. I have not met anyone I fancied to go out on date with and just going out with someone for going out is a complete waste of time. I can go out all by myself.”

“I agree with you,” he told her briefly. “Will you be okay in here by yourself? I have something to finish up in my office. You can come in when you are finished.”

Janice stared after him. He looked so solitary and lonely; she thought and somehow wished she could erase the sad look from his face. With a shrug she started working. She had sent over the arrangements from this morning and had found some clear bowls to place the flowers inside as well. She had come armed with some Sprite and hairspray to do the trick of making the plants last longer.

She was finished in half an hour and decided to find his office. She had asked him if he did not need floral arrangements for any of the offices including his and he had told her he would think about it. His door was open and she could see his dark head bent over a tablet, his brow creased in concentration. “I hope I am not disturbing you.”

He looked up immediately and put aside the device. “Not at all. You are all finished?”

“I am if you would like to take a look,” she suggested.

“I trust your judgment,” he said with a smile. “And besides you are the expert.”

“I hope there is someone here who will remember to change the water every two days or they tend to wilt.” Janice took a seat in front of his desk.

“I was thinking about that. Do you think we could get fresh arrangements every three days?”

Janice looked at him in surprise, her heart racing! It was exactly what she had hoped for!

“I definitely could do that,” she told him, trying to appear casual but not quite succeeding.

“And I would also like arrangements to be put in all the offices as well. Think you can handle that?” He was leaning back in his chair and looking at her quizzically.

“I will be happy to do so. Thank you,” she told him.

“You are welcome. My dad was not into bright colors and preferred an office to look like an office, but I must say the addition of a touch of color makes the surroundings much more pleasant and comfortable to be in.”

“It most certainly does,” Janice agreed, calculating the amount of money in her head. It was the biggest contract she had had since she had opened!

“Please make out the bill each week and send it to accounts.” He paused and stared at her. “Would you like to have dinner?”

Janice looked at him in amusement. “Don’t tell me, the chef left something for you in case you were hungry.”

“Something like that,” he said with a ghost of a smile.

“I would love to.” She nodded, wondering what on earth she was doing. She had some paperwork to finish and the spring festival was tomorrow afternoon, so she had to get to the location early to set up, but it was dinner and he was giving her a lot of business so surely she could take the time out to have dinner with him.

He picked up the phone and spoke briefly to someone before coming from around the desk.

“Pierre has smoked salmon and baby potatoes available. I hope that’s okay?”

“Sounds delicious.” She stood up and joined him around the table.

“White wine?” He held up a bottle already chilled.

“Thanks.”

He poured both glasses and came over to join her. She tasted it and her eyes widened in surprise. “This is really good!”

“It’s called La Sibilia,” he informed her. “I don’t much care for dryness myself.” He took a sip and put the glass down. “You said you are not dating, but don’t you get lonely?”

She tilted her head to one side as if thinking about his question. “I work long hours from Monday to Saturday and I have friends I socialize with. There is also my mother and father, we happen to have a good relationship. The only time I am usually by myself is on Sundays and sometimes I am at a function. I don’t get time to be lonely.”

There was a knock on the door just then and he beckoned for the person to come in. “Pierre, this is Janice Langley, she will be doing the floral arrangements for the company.” The man was a rotund balding Caucasian with a ruddy face and a beaming smile. He placed the tray in the middle of the table and whipped off the snowy white napkin.

“Nice to meet you. I have included my famous chocolate mousse and a pot of coffee.” With a bow, he left the room.

“This looks delicious.” She sniffed the air.

He stood up and passed a plate to her and put the next one over where he was sitting. They ate the meal in silence and

Janice found herself wondering if he was thinking about his wife. Did she have dinner with him at the office sometimes? Or did he take her out and then they go home together?

He poured the coffee into two very small cups and handed her a bowl of chocolate mousse.

“Pierre is very good,” she murmured, tasting the concoction and closing her eyes in pleasure.

He looked at her for a moment, his eyes drawn to her lips then he dragged his eyes away and looked down on his plate. “Yes, he is,” he said stiffly. They continued eating in silence and then finished their coffee.

“Are you going to stay and continue working?” she asked him, breaking the silence.

He was looking down into his coffee cup broodingly and when she spoke he looked up at her. “I think I will.”

“I know it is not my place because I only just met you, but I think it is time you start living again.”

He put down the cup and gave her his full attention and somehow Janice knew that she had probably said the wrong thing. “You think you know what I am going through?” His tone was soft but she could hear the steel behind it and wished she could take back what she had just said.

“I don’t and I am sorry,” she told him quietly, ready to leave.

He shrugged and stood up, waiting for her to do so as well. “I will see you out,” he told her.

Janice felt her heart sinking to the floor. She stopped at the door as they were heading out. “I am sorry, David,” She turned to face him, looking up at him with contrition. He stared down at her, his expression unreadable and for a moment there was a charge in the atmosphere. He was very tall; she only barely reached his shoulders. He saw her parted lips and her exquisite face and felt a stirring within him and knew he could never ask her to come here when he was alone again.

“That’s all right,” he told her casually, forcing himself to move away from her. Her nearness was getting to him.

She nodded and they rode the elevator in silence each wrapped up in their own thoughts.

*****

David went back into his office and was not surprised to notice that the plates had been cleared away from the table. He had stared at her and he had wanted to kiss her. He poured himself a stiff drink and downed the liquid hastily, coughing as he did so. His wife had died barely a year ago and here he was desiring another woman, what kind of monster was he.

His mind drifted back to the argument they had had a week before her death. “I love you, David!” she had cried. “What more do you want from me?”

“I want you to stop asking me about a child, Eileen. We are not ready for that sort of commitment yet.”

“When will we be ready, David?” she had asked him sadly. “When you decide if you will ever fall in love with me?”

“We are not going there, Eileen,” he had told her coldly. “You knew how I felt before we got married and you said you were prepared to deal with it.”

“It so happens that I have changed my mind. I love you and I want you to love me back.”

He had walked out of the room and left her, angry and frustrated at the nagging and angry with himself for not loving her.

He was doing penance and if it meant staying away from other women, then so be it!

*****

"I just love spring festivals, don't you?" Janice looked up from the leaves she was pruning on the stage and noticed that it was Mayor Sarah Logan. The middle aged African American woman had been mayor for the small town for a number of years and made it her duty to attend every one of the civic events. The weather was cool and beautiful with not a cloud to be seen. People were milling around and looking at the various arts and crafts on display and the food carts were scattered all around the park

"Hi Mayor Logan," she greeted the friendly woman warmly.

"Your flowers look magnificent and healthy as usual, Janice," she said with a beam, waving to some people who were calling to her.

"Thank you." She had left Maggie at the shop and she and Jake had come out to the festival. There was going to be a concert later and a pie judging contest but she doubted she was going to stay for the entire thing.

It was already one o'clock and she felt her belly rumbling reminding her that apart from the plain bagel and coffee she had had this morning she had not eaten anything else.

She excused herself and went to one of the stands to get a hot dog and something to drink. There was no sign of Jake and she suspected he was at some of the booths decorating. "Here you go Janice, on the house," Mickey said with a flourish handing her a hotdog with everything on it.

"Mickey, no." She gave a token protest but took it just the same. They did that all the time and he would insist that he was not taking a cent from her. She usually made up for it by sending some children to get something for themselves on her.

She ate and walked, looking at the displays and the arrangements she had put up at strategic places. She turned around when she heard her name and waved her friends over. Leah had the day off and both she and Candace had decided to come out since Janice was going to be there. Her mother had also said she was going to be there as well.

“Lord I am suddenly wishing I had stayed home and sleep the day away,” Leah complained transferring her large pocketbook from one shoulder to the next.

“Don’t listen to her, she just wanted to stay home and have sex with Lance,” Candace said dryly. Both of them were in knee length shorts and light sweaters. Janice had worn a khaki pants and a light pink blouse with a tan sweater vest.

“So what’s wrong with that?” Leah asked her.

“Cut it out you two,” Janice said mildly, linking her arms between them and heading to a costume jewelry booth.

*****

“I thought you were going to the spring festival,” Richard said lazily, trailing a finger down her naked torso. He had come by for breakfast and had not left yet. He was fascinated by the fact that he was enjoying her company more now than when they were married and wished he felt guilty about cheating on

Charlene, but he could not work up the effort. He had told her he had work to do and had headed over to his ex-wife's place.

"Why don't we go together?" Janet asked him teasingly.

"Are you crazy?" he asked her shocked. "That place is filled with nosy people and besides our daughter and her friends will be there."

"What about that two-year-old you are engaged to?" she asked him with a lifting of her finely arched brow.

"Be nice," he told her mildly. "She might be there as well." His hand drifted down to her pubic area and she opened her legs readily. "I doubt we will be leaving here for awhile," he whispered as he pushed his fingers inside her.

*****

David smiled and said all the right things. Pierre had outdone himself in the catering department and the center piece on the table had elicited quite a number of comments but it meant that the flowers reminded him of her and the way she smelled and the way she had looked up at him. She had told him she had a spring festival to attend and she was going to working as well and he wished he could just ditch his responsibilities and go out and mingle and see her work. He had not slept much last night but had twisted and turned in the huge bed restlessly.

He left the room discreetly and went inside his office just to get away from the people there and sat there around his desk. She had told him to let go of the past and start living again, but she had no idea what he was holding onto. He had never been one for socializing even before he had married Eileen and now it had gotten worse. How could he start living when he doubted he ever knew how?

*****

Charlene let the gossip flow over her head as she styled the hair in front of her. She was far away and it was a wonder she could concentrate on what she was doing. He had told her he had work to do, but she knew he was lying. He had not had sex with her in two weeks and when she asked why he had told her that he was very tired and he was not in the mood; that translated that he was getting it elsewhere.

“Charlene dear, how is the planning of the wedding coming on?” the woman whose hair she was styling asked her. Mrs.

Eldridge had been her customer for a number of years and had told her quite bluntly that for a man to spend so many years with a woman and suddenly decide that he wanted to be with someone else was not practical. They tend to go back to their wives, she had told her.

“It’s going,” she said trying to sound cheerful.

“When is the wedding?”

Charlene was aware that all conversations had ceased in the busy salon and all eyes were on her. “Sometime in June,” she said brightly.

“Are you sure that man is over his wife?” a particularly hateful elderly woman asked. Her name was Laura Gibbons and she was the town’s busybody.

“Of course he is,” Charlene answered sharply.

“If you say so,” she said smugly as if she knew something Charlene did not know.

She continued to style the hair, her brain working rapidly.

*****

“I think I put my foot in my mouth,” Janice told them wryly. They were standing by the refreshment booth sampling strawberry shortcake. The crowd had swelled dramatically and she had sent Jake back to the store to help out Maggie who had been overrun with customers. She had not seen any sign of her mother so far, and she was planning on leaving there at three o’clock.

“Don’t you always?” Candace said teasingly.

“I don’t,” Janice protested, waving to several of her mother’s neighbors.

“Did you apologize?” Leah asked her, brushing away the crumbs and icing from her hands.

“I did, two times, but somehow I think it was not quite enough.”

“Poor guy,” Leah sad sympathetically. “In my line of work you tend to see these tragedies all the time,” she said with a sigh.

“Are you staying for the show?” Candace asked Janice.

“Can’t, I have to go back to the store. Oh, there is Mom. I thought she was not coming.”

“She looks flushed and radiant,” Leah commented. “That can only mean one thing,” she whispered.

“Don’t say it,” Janice warned, smiling as her mother came nearer, looking around to see if her father was there.

“Hello girls,” she greeted the trio warmly. She was dressed in green linen pants and a light white sweater with her hair caught up on top of her head and secured by a white jeweled clip. “I had some things to take care of before I got here.”

“Hi, Mrs. Langley,” Candace and Leah greeted her. “You look nice,” Leah added.

“Thanks dear,” she said with a smile.

“We are going to take a look at the entertainment going on over there.” Leah pointed in the opposite direction where a crowd had gathered. “We will catch up later.”

“Mom, are you okay?” she asked as the woman and linked her arm through hers.

“Of course darling, why wouldn’t I be?” She waved to several people and looked around in excitement. “Spring always makes me feel light and happy; I guess it's the smell of the flowers and the coolness of the weather."

"Have you seen Dad?" Janice asked her casually.

"Why?" Janet stopped, forcing her to do so as well.

"I was just wondering,"

"I saw him this morning honey; we are kind of seeing each other again."

Chapter 4

"Dad, I don't want to hear it!" Janice exclaimed. She had just reached home from the store and had propped her tired feet onto an ottoman and settled back in the sofa with a much needed glass of red wine to relax her. It had been a week since the spring festival and a week since her mother had told her that she was seeing her ex-husband again. She had not heard from or seen David since, even when she had gone to his office building to change he floral arrangements on Thursday. His secretary had smilingly told her that she loved the smell of fresh flowers when she came in during the morning.

Janice had put alliums and begonias in his office. Not on his desk but on a beautiful cherry wood table in the corner of the room and the table where they had had their meals.

She had to admit that she missed seeing him.

"Baby girl, I want you to understand that I did not set out for this to happen, it just did," he told her contritely.

"So what are planning to tell the woman you are engaged to?"

"It's not like you ever warmed up to her, honey," he said trying to reason with her. "And I am not planning to tell her anything just yet."

"I could never warm up to her because she is only three years my senior and you never brought her around," his daughter reminded him.

"I know honey," he said with a sigh. "I think she is starting to suspect something."

"Think?" Janice said with a wry laugh. "You are spending a lot of time at Mom's so it would be safe to say she already knows."

"Your old dad has gotten himself into quite a pickle," he said with a wry laugh.

"I think you have."

"Okay baby girl, I will talk to you later."

"Bye Dad," she said softly hanging up from him.

She was just finishing the glass of wine when her phone rang again. She frowned at the unfamiliar number. "Hello?"

“Janice?” the familiar deep voice asked her.

“This is she.” Her heart had picked up speed.

“It’s David Hattori,” he responded. “I hope I have not called you too late.”

“No.” She closed her eyes briefly. “I just not too long got in from the store. How are you?”

“I am okay, thank you,” he said politely. “I want to thank you for the arrangements. I loved the colors you chose for my office.”

“I am happy you like them,” she told him gently.

He went silent for a spell and she waited on him to speak again. “How was the fair?’ he finally asked her.

“It was interesting,” she told him with a laugh. She told him about the various events.

“I wished I had been there,” he said softly.

“I wished you had been there too,” she heard herself saying. There was silence again and Janice wondered if she had said the wrong thing again.

“I have something to finish up so I will talk to you some other time.” His voice had gone cool and Janice felt frustration blooming. She liked him and she knew he was mourning, but she felt there was something there.

“David?”

“Yes?”

“You want to come over for dinner at my place?”

The silence stretched for so long that if she had not heard the open connection she would have thought he had hung up.

“I can’t,” he finally told her. “I am sorry.”

“Why?” She was not willing to let it go this time.

“Why what?” He sounded confused and for a minute Janice felt sorry for him.

“Why not dinner? I am just asking you to have dinner with me, a meal between people. I am not asking you to take me to bed, David,” she told him.

“I have to go.” He hung up on her.

Janice hung up with a grimace. He most definitely would not be calling her back!

*****

David found himself breathing hard. He could not believe that she had spoken to him that way! He had been thinking about her too much over the past week so he had gone out of his way to avoid her. He had even made sure he was not there when she got there with the arrangements. He had gone back to visit Eileen’s grave to try and get her out of his thoughts, but that had not work at all. He was constantly thinking about her and he need to stop. Now she had mentioned sex to him and had made the feeling worse! What was he going to do, he thought in despair.

*****

“Ah, here he is finally,” Julie said with relief as soon as he entered through the doorway. His eyes narrowed as they zeroed in on the woman seated in the living room with his mother. Her name was Arianna and she had made her intentions clear from the get go that she would not mind hooking up with him. By the looks of things, they were having pre dinner drinks and he was sorry he had not followed his mind and stayed at the office. Now he was going to be forced to have dinner and make small talk with a woman he was not in the least bit interested in. “Darling, I thought I would have to send out a search party for you,” his mother said brightly, deliberately ignoring the look she gave him.

“Mother,” his voice was cool, his eyes going to the woman who was giving her one of her seductive smiles. Even if he was not in the situation he found himself in, she would not have been his type; she was not his type, too obvious. “Arianna, how are you?” he asked her politely.

“Better now,” she purred, her sultry voice getting on his nerves.

“I am going to get washed up and then come back down. Mother, I need your help with something,” he said turning to leave the room. Julie had no choice but to follow him.

He was taking off his suit jacket and hanging it up when she came in.

“I don’t appreciate being railroaded, Mother,” he told her in a freezing tone. “I am tired after a very long day at the office and when I am ready to start dating again, I am perfectly able to pick out my own date.”

“Can you blame me?” She sat on the edge of the bed, and spread her arms. “You look like a ghoul each day and you are not eating properly. You spend most of the time at the office and you look as if you want to give up on life. You did not love her, David, and you were not the one who killed her, so let go and start living again please! I want my son back.”

He stood there staring at her, his hands clenched at his sides. “You and Dad interfered in my life once before and caused this,” he gritted. “I marry a woman I did not love and ended up destroying both our lives and now you are starting to do it again, it ends here.” He put his jacket back on and headed towards the door to the back stairway.

“Where are you going?” his mother asked in alarm following behind him.

“I am going out.” He flung the door behind him and headed for one of the cars parked in the circular driveway. It was drizzling, but he did not even notice. He was so angry that he was shaking! He was trying to recover from the debacle that had been his life before and now she was doing it all over again! He drove, not caring where he was going until his eyes cleared and he realized that he was heading back to the office. He parked outside and sat there in the car, leaning back against the headrest and closing his eyes. He heard his phone ringing and ignored it, sure that it was his mother calling.

His mind drifted unwillingly to one of the few happy times he had spent with Eileen. She had called him while he was at the office and told him she had a surprise for him and he should hurry up and come home. He had done so and she had lit candles and prepared sweet-and-sour pork and there was a small cake with his name on it. It had been his birthday and he had forgotten all about it because of some crises at the office.

“Happy birthday,” she had told him softly and led him to the chair to sit. She had told him to blow out the candle and he had done so. They had spent a very pleasant afternoon together.

He picked up his phone and dialed her number. It was almost nine o’clock and he was wondering if she had gone to bed. “Hello?”

“I am sorry to disturb you so late,” he said soberly.

“Will you stop apologizing?” she asked impatiently. “Are you okay?”

“I want to come over for a little bit.”

“Come on over,” she said without hesitation and gave him the address.

*****

He got there in fifteen minutes and she opened the door as soon as she saw him through the window. Her house faced a woodland area and was kind of isolated. It had belonged to her grandmother who had left it to her when she died. It was a rambling farm-type residence with a big yard and wide spaces and she loved it even though it was too big for one person.

He looked like hell, she thought sympathetically, closing the door behind him. His dark hair was damp from the drizzle and his shirt was damp.

"How about some tea?" she suggested, turning to go into the kitchen. She was behaving as if it was everyday she entertained a billionaire inside her house in her track bottom and tank top. She had gone jogging after he had hung up on her to get her head cleared and she had not too long ago gotten back.

He nodded and to her surprise he came into the kitchen with her. The kitchen was large and homey and still had the old fashioned range her grandmother had used in her day. Janice had added a brand new stove but had kept the range, saying that it gave the place character.

"Herbal or chamomile?" she asked him looking in the pantry.

"It doesn't matter," he told her, wondering what he was doing here.

“Herbal it is then.” She put on the kettle and took down two cups.

He was sitting on one of the stools with his hands clasped in front of him on the counter. “This is a nice place,” he murmured, looking around.

“It belonged to my grandparents and my grandma left it to me two years ago when she died,” she told him.

“You were close to her.” He said it like a statement.

“I was her only grandchild, so yes,” she told him with a smile, turning off the knob and pouring some water in both mugs, passing one to him.

“I guess you are wondering what I am doing here.” He stared down at the brown liquid in his cup as if he could find answers in there.

“You are drinking tea with me,” she told him with a wicked smile, sipping her tea.

He looked up and was caught by her dazzling smile. Her hair was tied up in a pigtail with several tendrils escaping and lying on her cheeks. “My mother had a woman over.”

"I see," she looked at him quizzically, one well shaped brow arched. "And you had to get out of there because she was so unattractive."

His mouth lifted in a slight smile. "Exactly," he said softly. His gaze drifted to somewhere behind her head. "My marriage was arranged and I never loved my wife. Our families thought it was natural for us to get married, to join both families together. I was against it at first, but I was caught up in it and before I knew it was agreeing to it. I tried to love her but I could not." He stopped and looked so tortured that she just wanted to hold him and tell him that everything was going to be okay.

"You are feeling guilty for not returning her feelings," she said quietly. His tea was getting cold, she observed objectively.

He gave her a wintry smile. "She wanted us to have children, but I callously asked her if it was wise to bring children into a loveless marriage."

Janice felt sorry for a wife who desperately wanted her husband's love any way she could get it and for him and the burden of guilt he was facing.

“There is nothing you can do now to change it, David, and if she had been alive, you two would have probably ended up being divorced.” She walked around to his side and he turned to face her. “You are killing yourself with the guilt and it’s not doing you any good. You are going to have to find a way to move away from it and start living again otherwise you are going to be in a bad place for the rest of your life.” She reached up and touched his strong jaw, trying to ease the rigidity she saw there.

Her touch had an explosive effect on him! With a tortured groan, he pulled her inside the circle of his arms, his hands framing her face. He stared down at her for a moment and then he bent his head but he did not have to go too far because she met his lips halfway, burying her fingers into his now dry hair. His tongue touched hers tentatively and she trembled as the passion raced through her inexperienced body. She wanted to make him forget, she wanted to make him think about her and forget the guilt.

David deepened the kiss, the feelings that had lain dormant for so many years springing forth. He had never felt this way before, not with anyone and he was confused. He tore his mouth away from hers and put her away from him, springing from the stool.

“I am sorry,” he muttered harshly, shoving his fingers through his hair. His erection was obvious for her to see and it was also very painful.

“Stop!” She made a move towards him and he stepped back. “Oh David, when are you to let yourself feel again?”

“I need to go.” He looked around the room as if looking for somewhere to hide. “I have to go.” He headed for the door and Janice walked behind him. He turned and looked at her for a minute, his dark eyes burning her flesh as he took in her swollen lips and her slumberous eyes and her nipples stiff against the thin shirt and then with a tortured groan he slammed out of the house.

*****

His mother was waiting for him when he got home. He had driven around the back and gone up the back staircase, but she was waiting for him in the hallway.

“I can’t do this now, Mother,” he told her grimly, heading towards his suite.

“I want to apologize to you,” she told him softly, following behind him.

“I need to get some sleep. I have an early meeting tomorrow.” He slipped out of his jacket and hung it over the railing of the bed.

“This won’t take long.”

With a sigh, he turned to face her.

“You were right,” she told him quietly. “Your father and I interfered and we somehow managed to convince you that marrying Eileen was a good plan for both families, not thinking about how you felt.” She sighed. “I am sorry, David. I see you going through your agony and I cannot do anything to help you and it makes me feel as if I have failed you as a mother.”

He came and sat beside her. “I went into it willingly, Mother, so I am to be blamed as well,” he told her quietly.

“I just need my son back that’s all,” she told him softly.

“It will happen eventually.” He looked at her. “What happened to Arianna?”

“I told her that something urgent came up at the office and you had to rush out,” his mother said with a faint smile. “I am not quite sure she believed me.”

David laughed at her woebegone expression. “She was never my type, Mother.”

“I am beginning to realize.” She reached out and rested her hand on his strong jaw. “I hope you find someone who loves you and you feel the same,” she murmured.

“I am not ready for that yet,” he told her, his heart skidding as he remembered what he had just shared with Janice. He put it from his mind firmly, determined not to go there!

*****

“What is going on, Richard?” Charlene demanded. They were in his living room and she had just left the salon determined to have it out with him. He was going to tell her the truth even if she had to wait him out. “Who is she?”

He felt his heart pounding. He had been on his way over to see his ex-wife when she showed up unexpectedly. Today was Saturday and was supposed to be the busiest day at the salon, so she was not supposed to be here and she had not called.

“Why do you think there is a she?” he asked her mildly.

“Well let’s see?” she pretended to consider. “You have not had sex with me in two weeks, you keep telling me that you have to work, and I have not heard anything about our wedding. Have I left anything out?”

“Look Charlene,” he said with a sigh, wondering how on earth he had landed himself in this position. He was fifty four years old and he should not have to deal with all this drama in his life. “I think we should slow it down a little bit. I need to do some thinking.”

“You are leaving me?” Charlene felt as if he had taken a knife to her heart, the pain was that sharp.

“I am not leaving you, I just need some space that’s all,” he said soothingly.

“That translates to mean that you want out and you don’t know how to say it.” Her lips were trembling and she was fighting the tears.

“I am not leaving you,” he said impatiently, hating scenes. “I just need some time that’s all. I am sorry.”

“You bastard!” she screamed and grabbed up her pocket book, slamming the door behind her.

He flopped down on the sofa wearily, then got up to lock the door, not sure if in her irrational mood, Charlene wouldn’t return with a gun to blow his brains out. What a mess!

His phone rang just then and his lips curved into a smile. “Have you told her?” Janet asked him.

“Sort of,” he said ruefully. “I told her I needed space.”

“Oh Lord Richard, that to her means you want out and now,” Janet told him. “You could not have been more subtle?”

“I thought you wanted me to get rid of her?” he asked her incredulously, never for one minute understanding how women think.

"Of course I do, but you don't want her to come after you, do you?" she asked him silkily.

"You think she will?" he asked in concern.

"Hell hath no fury like a woman scorned darling," she reminded him.

"Thanks, that's all I needed."

*****

Janice wanted to call him but she knew he was not going to talk to her. She could not believe he was suffering guilt! She had thought he was in love with her and she was wondering how she was going to compete with that. She touched her lips and still felt his on hers, his tongue in her mouth. She shivered as she remembered how she had felt in his arms and knew she wanted more of him. How was she going to convince him that they needed each other? That they would be good together? She had never been in a relationship before, apart from exchanging a few kisses with boys in college, that had been it for her and those kisses had been pleasant but not earth shaking. David Hattori had showed her a different side and had lit a fire inside her that could only be quenched by him. She stood underneath the shower and allowed the water to beat down on her from her head down, her eyes closed as she remembered what kissing him felt like!

Chapter 5

“We are going clubbing tonight and I don’t want to hear another word about it,” Candace told them firmly. “There is a new club that opened up downtown and we are going to dance, pick up men, and drink strong liquors.”

Janice had started to protest but she had decided against it. She had not heard from David and she had not called him even though she had been aching for him.

So now she was getting ready to go with her friends. It was a little after eight and she had bought an outfit to wear tonight. Candace was right, instead of sitting at home pining for a man she could not have, she needed to get out there and have fun. The skirt was very short and she paired it with a long black shirt, leggings and knee length black boots. She had let her hair loose for a change and had used the flat iron to straighten her shoulder length black hair and it swung softly against her face. She had applied more make-up than usual and a bright red lipstick that highlighted her full lips. She grabbed her house keys and pocket book and headed for the door. She had decided to take a cab to meet her friends at the club as they had planned not to drive.

“Point me to the nearest bar,” Leah exclaimed. She had had an argument with Lance who been upset that she was going to a club instead of spending time with him. “I need to get the taste of the argument of Lance out of my mind.” She had on snug fitting black denim and a red and white silk blouse. Candace was wearing close fitting red dress with a plunging neckline. The three girls turned many heads as they wove their way through the crowd towards the bar.

“He wants to tie me down and I am not supposed to go anywhere without him.” Leah said taking a sip of her Smirnoff Ice. The other two had ordered the same. “I told him that we are in the middle of filing for a divorce so I did not want to hear a peep out of him.”

“Jeremy told me yesterday that I was not his type, he needed someone more career oriented,” Candace told them downing the strong liquor and almost choked in the process.

“Oh honey!” Janice patted her back gently. “He is not worth you pining over him. I have been telling myself that since David left the house in a hurry. Let him stay wrapped up in his guilt for his dead wife. What do I care?”

“Ouch sweetie, that sounds a little harsh,” Candace told her with a grimace.

“I know and that is not me.” She downed the liquid in her glass and felt the heat go through her body.

“Okay you know what?” Leah said signaling the waiter for another round. “We are here to forget about men and that is exactly what we are going to do.”

They danced with some brothers who had been busily checking them out, and by the middle of the night they were comfortably drunk.

“I can’t believe you are single.” His name was Derek and he was holding her way too close and his cologne was very overpowering. Her friends were dancing as well with two guys; it was obvious that they had come together.

“Why is that?” Janice asked him faintly, she was finding it hard to breathe. His cologne combined with the heat of the club was making her dizzy.

“You are one fine looking woman,” he said leeringly, one hand drifting down to her bottom.

“Let your hand wander down there again and I knee you in the groin,” she told him grimly.

“Okay baby, just checking out the shape.” He grinned at her and suddenly she felt sick, just wanting to get out of his totally uncomfortable embrace. The song ended just then and she pulled away quickly but he held on to her. “How about coming back to my place? I am willing to show you a good time.”

“I strongly doubt that,” she told him sarcastically, pulling her hand away from him and walking away.

“You don’t know what you are missing honey,” he called after her.

“What was that all about?” Leah asked her as soon as she sat at the table. They had ordered something to eat to soak up the liquor they had been drinking. Janice dunked her fries into the thick ketchup and looked back at where her dance partner was over at the bar with his friends looking over at them.

“He wanted to show me a good time at his place,” Janice said mildly. Her head was spinning and her stomach was roiling but she figured the chicken and chips would make it better.

“And you let an offer like that pass you by?” Leah said teasingly.

“Mine wanted to know if I was available for a ménage a trois,” Candace said with an irrepressible grin.

“No!” Leah covered her mouth to keep from laughing out loud. “I missed all the fun. Mine just wanted to hold my delectable body in his arms for the entire night.”

They laughed softly at that and settled back to finish the meal.

There was a dancing contest going on stage with two females and two males and the disc jockey played reggae music to start off the contest. The girls found themselves standing to get a better view and watched in wonder at the dance moves that were showed.

It was the last round that did it. It was approaching eleven o’clock and they went back to the bar to order one last round. Their avid admirers had found other women and had not given them another glance. “Vodka and tonic, please,” Leah told the bartender.

“I am not sure I can manage that,” Janice protested.

“It’s the last drink for the night,” Leah insisted.

They ended up having two drinks and by that time Janice’s head was spinning! Her friend’s helped her into the cab and told the driver where to take her.

*****

“It was almost midnight when she stumbled out of the cab and pulled open her gate. She made it to the porch before dropping on one of the chairs there, her head pounding. Oh God! She felt like she was dying. What on earth had possessed her to drink so much when she did not have the stomach for it? Fishing inside her pocket book she took out her phone and dialed his number. “Hello?” His voice sounded sleepy and she felt elated that she had woke him from his peaceful sleep.

“Hi David.” Her voice was slurred and she struggled to sound normal.

“Janice?” He sounded wide awake now.

“I bet you are wondering why I am calling you so late. I bet you are wondering why I am calling you at all.” She bent her head and took several deep breaths. “I am just coming from – I was just at a club having a good time.” She laughed suddenly, almost hysterically.

“Janice, are you drunk?”

“Am I drunk? Let’s see,” she giggled. “I guess I am. I met some guy and we danced and he wanted to take me to his place to have sex with me.”

He was wide awake now.”Janice, where are you?”he asked her urgently.

“What do you care?” she asked him in an annoyed voice. “You are at home in your comfortable home wrapped up in guilt about your dead wife, so what the hell do you care?” Her lids were closing and her stomach felt queasy. “You are quite fine, David, you don’t need a real live woman beside you. There is your dead wife right there, so I guess, I mean I – You know what? I don’t know what the hell I am saying. Goodbye David, and have a nice life.” She hung up and allowed the phone to fall to the floor and rested her head on the chair, her eyes closing in drunken sleep.

*****

That was where he found her half an hour later. He had almost killed himself coming over and had wondered what the hell she had done to herself. He had not called her and had made sure he was not around when she came to replace the floral arrangements. But she was right. He was using Eileen's death as a crutch for his guilt and because he was confused at the feelings she had evoked inside him, he did not know what to do. She was slumped over in an uncomfortable position on the porch chair. He stood there looking at her for a moment before climbing the steps and coming closer to her. He shook her gently and called her name, but she did not budge. It took him ten minutes before he was able to wake her and she stirred, looking at him crouched beside her. "David?" she murmured, one hand reaching out to touch his jaw. "Am I dreaming?"

"No," he told her tightly. "I need to get you inside. Where are your keys?"

She pointed to her pocketbook.

He found the keys and opened the door and helped her up, guiding her inside. She gripped his hands as she felt her head spinning and the nausea coming up from inside her. "I am going to be sick!" she gasped. He hurried with her to the bathroom and she collapsed in front of the toilet bowl and puked her guts out. He held her hair back, and when she was finished she leaned back against him weakly. "I am going to die."

"Alcohol will do that to you anytime," he said grimly, helping her up and walking with her to the sink to rinse out her mouth.

He guided her into the bedroom and proceeded to undress her. She put up a token resistance and he boxed away her hands and continued. "I don't make love to drunken women Janice," he told her tightly. She let him and dropped on the bed as he pulled a t-shirt over her head and pulled the sheets over her body. By the time he came back from the kitchen where he had made her a cup of tea, she was out like a light.

He stood there looking at her. He had undressed her and had tried to ignore the tightening of his body as he stared at her generous breasts, the large nipples apparent in their lace casing. She had on matching panties and he had found himself aching to touch her there. Her skin was so soft and beautiful and he imagined himself tasting every inch of it. He had had to force himself from pulling her into his arms and kissing her. She was dangerous to his senses and that was why he had stayed away from her. He pulled up a chair and sat, deciding to drink the tea himself and stayed there watching her sleep until he drifted off.

*****

She woke up groggy and with a blinding headache. The sun was streaming in through the partially opened curtains in her room and she felt the light straight into her skull. It was then she smelled coffee. With a groan she tentatively got off the bed. What the hell happened to her? And who was making coffee?

He came in just then and Janice looked up at him in shock. What was David doing here?

“I see you are up.” He brought in a tray with the enticing smell of freshly brewed coffee and two pills on a saucer. He brought them over to her.

“What are you doing here?” she croaked, automatically reaching for the aspirins and popping them inside her mouth, using the coffee to swallow them down.

“You called me last night and told me all about your night,” he told her coolly. He took the tray away and took a seat on the chair. “Do you often get drunk like that?”

She shook her head and winced as the pain laced though her temple. “Never. What did I say to you?”

“You told me that you met some man who wanted to have sex with you and I should stay home in my comfortable bed wrapped in the guilt of losing my wife,” he told her in a matter of fact tone, his eyes holding hers.

“Oh Lord.” She closed her eyes in mortification. “I am sorry, David.”

“I came over and found you spread out on the porch chair fast asleep.”

“You undressed me?”

He nodded.

“Did we-?” She could not even bring herself to say the word.

"You mean did we have sex?" he asked her with a tinge of amusement. "No, I don't take advantage of incapacitated women." He stood up then. "Are you going to be all right?"

She nodded and noticed that the headache was wearing off.

"I will be leaving then and if I may suggest, you monitor your intake of alcohol from now on." He turned to leave.

"That's it?" She stood up a little unsteadily. "You are leaving?"

"What do you want me to do, Janice?" His back was still turned to her. "You want me to stay and hold your hand?"

"Damn you, David!" she cried in frustration. "Leave and don't come back. Do what you know best, run away from what you are feeling because you are too much of a coward to acknowledge that you can actually feel." The silence that followed her outburst was deafening and from the clenching of his fists she knew she had gone too far!

He turned to face her and she saw his dark eyes flashing with anger. She stood her ground as he came forward, her body trembling slightly. "What are you doing?" he asked her softly, his hands gripping her arms with bruising force.

"David-" she began, putting up her hands to hold him off.

"Damn you!" he muttered pulling her towards him. "Damn you." His head came down and he took her lips with a hunger and force that took her breath away. She opened her mouth underneath his, her hands going around his neck bringing him even closer. His tongue invaded her mouth and he crushed her against him, his heart hammering inside his chest. She returned the kiss with aching ardor, molding herself to him as he plundered her mouth helplessly.

With a swift movement he lifted her into his arms and bore her back against the bed placing her there gently. He released her lips and she moaned wanting to feel him. "Hush," he whispered. He pulled the shirt over her head and then took off her bra and panties. He knelt there staring at her breasts with their generous nipples and knew he had to taste them. He bent his head and took a nipple inside his mouth, pulling it, his tongue swirling around it. Janice gasped and stiffened against him, the need racing through her already vulnerable body. He went to her other nipple and by the time he was finished she was a quivering mass of desire. He eased off the bed and hurriedly undressed leaving on his underwear but she could see his erection straining against the material. He opened her legs and used his fingers to open the lips of her vagina. His eyes captured hers as he put his finger inside her, thrusting slowly, watching her reaction. He used his other hand to release his erection and her eyes were drawn to it and she whimpered helplessly at the length and width of him. He took the finger out and rubbed it against the tip of him using it to lubricate his penis. He was still silent, still watching her and Janice found herself shivering at his look. He came onto the bed and guided his erection into her, his teeth gritted as he encountered her incredible tightness. He pushed further and her barrier stopped him. “You are a virgin?” he asked her harshly, making as if to pull out of her.

Janice wrapped her legs around his waist, keeping him inside her. “I need this,” she whispered.

With a groan he pushed against her, stopping again at her brief cry of pain. He pushed further and breached her capturing her cry inside his mouth. He waited until she had become accustomed to him before moving against her. She matched him, thrust for thrust, her arms around his neck, her body on fire for him. The sensation was incredible! David gathered her up against him and gripping her hips he increased the pace, his breathing labored.

He had never before in his life experienced such a passion. It was overwhelming and threatened to tear at his control, a control that he had always exercised and always kept in check. He had known that she was different when he first met her but he had never dreamed of how much. He felt his penis burgeoning inside her, hugging the walls of her vagina and holding him to her, clinging and melting his reservations and the feelings of coldness and aloofness he had always had.

Janice tore her mouth from his and with a sharp cry she came against him, her body trembling uncontrollably. He came with her, while she was in the throes of ecstasy and his fingers gripped her hips as he thrust inside her desperately, furiously, his body increasing the pace and taking over.

They clung to each other as they rode the storm together still holding each other as they drifted back down.

He tried easing out of her, but she would not let him, her arms tightening around his taut lean body as she placed butterfly kisses on his bare muscled chest.

“Janice,” he groaned, moving inside her. He was still hard and he discovered that he wanted more, he had to have more of her, God help him!

“I want you to stay,” she did not know what she as asking, whether it was to stay the day of for the entire time but she knew she could not let him go, not now, not ever.

He bent his head and took her lips with his softly. She responded and tunneled her fingers through his soft dark hair as her tongue met his eagerly. She met his movements with hers and loved the feel of him inside her soaking wet vagina. The sun had gone behind a dark cloud and it had started raining but they did not notice, neither of them noticed or even heard the ringing of the phone as they lose themselves into each other, their bodies eagerly giving and receiving.

*****

It was David who woke up first. He had eased out of her when she had drifted off into an exhausted sleep and had gathered her close to him and gone to sleep himself. Her body was curled against his, her hand curled into fist on his chest. He moved away gently and looked down at her exquisite face still bearing the effects of their passionate time together. He had gone down on her, licking at her mound and pulling it inside his mouth until she had sobbed and asked him for release. He had used his tongue to give her release, thrusting inside her with an expertise that had had her panting. It was then and only then that he had taken her again, placing his penis inside her and screwing her hurriedly, his breathing harsh against her mouth. Just looking at her made hard and he wondered how on earth he could feel such intensity for a woman he had not too long met.

He noticed how long her lashes were, and the shadows they made against her soft cheeks and her lips partially opened as she breathed evenly in sleep.

He had wanted to leave and have nothing to do with her. What he felt for her was nothing compared to what he had felt for any other woman including the one he had marry and it made the guilt inside him even worse!

She stirred against him and opened her eyes. “I thought I was having a particularly erotic dream,” she murmured, lifting a hand to touch his jaw.

“It’s very real,” he told her lightly, knowing he should probably head on home and run as far away as possible.

“I know,” she reached between them and held his penis lightly, drifting down to the tip of him where she rubbed her finger over the slight wetness. “This is very real and I want more.” He had hardened visibly as she continued to stroke him and he could feel his body tighten in desire.

“Janice,” he murmured achingly and sliding on top of her he entered her swiftly, going in deep.

She wrapped her legs around his waist and lifted her hips, giving as good as she got!

Chapter 6

He did not call her the next day. He had left late in the afternoon after they had eaten and had made love again, his hands roaming her body feverishly, his lips touching hers and lingering. He had not promised to call her, but she had thought that after sharing something so unbelievably wonderful that he would have at least called.

“Hi Janice, how are you today? I just wanted to check up on you after that wonderful and passionate time we had spent together exploring each other’s bodies,” she muttered, clipping the dried leaves from the dogwood tree. She had gone into the greenhouse like she normally did on a Monday and had left Maggie and Jake in the store to make deliveries and ring up sales. She needed to get her head on straight. Leah and Candace had finally called her yesterday after he had gone to find out if she was still alive and she had almost told them about the time she had spent with him. But it was too soon and too new.

She had soaked in a warm bath for a very long time after he had left, closing her eyes and feeling his body on hers. She wanted to feel it again and he was not going to stop her.

It was going on four in the afternoon when she decided to bite the bullet and call him. “Janice, how are you feeling?” His tone was polite, as if they had just met.

“Oh no, we are not doing that, David,” she told him in frustration. “We did not spend one whole afternoon making love and you taking my prized virginity for you to be treating me like some damned stranger.”

“I cannot do this now, Janice,” he told her tightly.

“Then when, David?” She placed the clipper she had been using down on the table and started pacing. “Because I am not going to let you go back to hiding behind your guilt, not after yesterday.”

“We had a very pleasant time yesterday, Janice, and I want to thank you for that, but I am not interested in a relationship,” he told her coldly.

“You want to thank me?” She could not believe he had just said that.

“I have a meeting,” he muttered and hung up the phone hurriedly.

Janice could not believe he had done that again. Okay mister, you think you can get rid of me that easily, think again!

*****

David was shaking. He replaced the phone on his desk and tunneled his hands through his usually very neat hair. He had left her place yesterday and driven along the countryside trying to think and he had come up empty. He had passed her house again and slowed down wanting to go back but he had flown past instead. He had not been able to sleep and thinking of her had made him so hard that he had had to stand underneath the icy cold shower to get some release. He kept picturing her and that made him uncomfortable and fired up. She had gotten under his skin and he had no idea what to do. His mother had wondered where he had gotten to and he had told her he had been at the office. She had looked at him strangely but had nodded, possibly accepting his explanation. He had also lied to Janice. There was no meeting he had to go to but he had had to get her off the phone.

What the hell was happening to him?

*****

“This is nice,” Janet murmured, sipping the wine and leaning back against her chair. She had invited Richard over for dinner and he had brought the wine with him. He had told her that he had not seen Charlene since he had told her he needed space and was hoping that was that.

“It is,” he murmured, gazing at her over his glass. She was truly a beautiful woman with a beautiful complexion. Her unruly curls had just a hint of grey and she had managed to catch them up neatly at the back of her neck. She had on a casual pink and white blouse and white knee length shorts and she looked very good. Why did he leave her? “I was thinking that I should give up my apartment and move back in.”

Janet almost choked on her wine. Yes, she enjoyed his company and it had suited her to steal him away from that home wrecker, but she had gotten used to her freedom and it felt liberating! Not that she did not love him; she did and always would, but she needed her space. His coming and going suited her just fine, but how was she going to tell him that?

"Sweetie, I think we should wait a little bit longer to sort out if that is what we really want," she suggested hastily.

"What are you saying?" He looked at her with narrowed eyes.

She got up from her place at the table and came over to where he was. She wiggled her way onto his lap and took the wine glass away from him. "We need to give it a little more time, this works for now so let's go with it." She unbuttoned her blouse and shrugged out of it, unhooking her bra and letting her still small breasts spring free for his greedy gaze. He pushed the chair back and turned her around to him, his fingers pinching her nipple causing the dart to sing through her and then bending his head he started sucking. He did not mention moving back in that evening, he was too distracted.

*****

Janice waited until she had closed the store and armed with a bouquet of flowers for the reception area, she headed out. She had called and made sure he would be at the office and the receptionist whom she had befriended had told her that he never left until very late. She smiled at the guard who sent her straight up. The place was empty as it should be at seven-thirty. She left the bouquet at the reception area and continued on her way to his office. His door was half opened and she saw the sliver of light from inside. His head was bent over a document when she pushed the door and entered. He looked up with a frown, his eyes narrowing when he saw it was her. She saw his hands tightening on the folder and hid a smile at his obvious reaction to her presence. “Have you eaten?” she asked him mildly.

“What?” He looked at her confused.

“Have you had dinner, David?” she asked again. He shook his head no.

“Good, we can call up Pierre and have him bring something in.” She walked over to his desk and pressed the buzzer to the kitchen. “Hi Pierre, how are you? Good, could you have something sent up to David’s office? Yes, I am joining him for dinner.” She released the buzzer and looked at him. He had not moved but was watching her as if he could not believe what she was doing.

“Shall we?” She indicated the table in the corner. She had brought a snowy white tablecloth and went to put it on the table, removing the vase of flowers and then putting it back, running a hand over the cloth. He had not moved, and he was not saying anything just watching her. With a sigh, she went back over to his desk and climbed onto his lap, unbuttoning the two top buttons of his red and white dress shirt. He reacted then, gripping her hands to stop her and then with a tortured groan, he dragged her head down to his, finding her mouth and plunging his tongue inside hungrily. His body shuddered against hers and she felt his erection against her. She moved on him and he pushed against her desperately. It was only when they heard the clatter of trays in the hallway that they sprang apart. Janice went to the door and pulled it open to give him enough time to pull himself together and greeted the smiling Pierre. “This looks delicious, Pierre, thank you.” The man left the tray of delicate seafood platter on the table and left.

David had left his desk and come up behind her. She was wearing a delicate pink and grey dress with horizontal strips that molded her figure lovingly and had on knee length boots. It was still cold even though spring was slowly drifting away, so she had put on leggings. He reached underneath her dress and pulled down her underwear, his hand spanning her smooth bottom before going under to find her vagina. Janice leaned back against him as his fingers found the core of her and dipped inside, thrusting quickly, She rode his fingers eagerly, her breath coming in short gasps, her heart beating loudly. He took his fingers from out of her and she heard his zipper going down and moaned as he bent her over the chair and took her forcibly from behind. He leaned against her, moving the wisps of curls from the nape of her neck and bit down on her softness none too gently as he thrust inside her hungrily. Janice cried out as the bolt shot through her and his hands gripped her hips, his thrusts seeking and desperate. He spilled inside her with a hoarse cry, his body bucking against hers and held her as she followed suit, her body moving against him frantically. Her leggings were ruined so she got rid of them and he cleaned her up with a piece of napkin, lingering against her.

They finally had dinner and it was halfway through that he asked her, “What are you doing?” His voice was quiet and his gaze was quizzical as he speared the lobster with his fork.

“I am eating.” She looked at him in surprise. “I thought you could see that.”

He gave her a wry look. His hair was messy and that was unusual for him. “You know what I mean, Janice.”

“No, actually I don’.” She put aside her fork and looked at him. “If you are referring to the fact that I am here now with you having dinner and the fact that you took me from behind just now then I will tell you that this is something that is happening between us and I am not going to let you run away from it.”

“I am not ready,” he muttered moodily, putting down his fork as well.

“Your body says otherwise,” she refuted. “I am not going anywhere, David, so get used to it and I am going to want to go out with you in public, maybe to a nice restaurant or to the movies or even to have a picnic in the park and make love with you over and over again, of course.”

“Stop it,” he groaned, pushing back his chair. “You are confusing me.” He had moved away from the table and went to stand by the window looking out. He looked so lost and alone and she had every intention of changing that. She followed him and stood before him.

“I am falling in love with you, David Hattori.” She slipped her hands around his neck, almost laughing at the shock on his handsome face.

“No,” he said achingly.

“Yes,” she responded firmly. “I am falling in love with you and there is absolutely nothing you can do about it.”

He stared down at her, taking in her soft full lips, her pert nose and her large dark brown eyes and knew he was in deep trouble. “Janice,” he whispered her name like a prayer.

“You are not going to avoid me as of now,” she told him softly. “I am not letting you do that anymore.”

With a helpless groan, he bent his head to feast off her lips, his hands tightening around her small waist.

*****

Charlene came to see her at the store on Friday. After the time at his office, he had started calling her. Still very polite and detached, but she knew it was just a shield and she did not pay it any mind. He came over to the house the next night and brought wine and they had dinner together after which he had made slow tender love to her, his mouth tasting and lingering on her body. She had wanted him to stay, but he had left. He had told her about work but nothing personal and only when they were making love did he let his guard down.

Her friends had called and invited her to go with them to a fashion show, but she had told them she had a date. “You are dating?” Leah had asked her suspiciously as if she suspected that Janice was just saying that to get out of hanging out with them.

“I am going out with David,” she had told them with a smile. He was taking her to a restaurant to have dinner.

“And a night of hot sex after?”Candace asked archly.

“Maybe.” She had told them what had happened the next day following the drunken binge they had indulged in the night before.

“Have fun!” Leah had told her.

She was preparing a floral arrangement to go out when the girl charged in. Maggie was attending to a customer and Jake had gone to make deliveries. They had weddings coming up in June and with the summer coming on very soon, flowers were in bloom.

“I need to talk to you,” the woman said in an undertone. Janice could not believe this was the same girl her father had shown her a few months ago; she looked haggard and the dark roots in her bottled blonde hair were very prominent.

“What can I do for you?” she asked, forcing her voice to be polite.

“Can we go around back?” she asked. Her mascara was running and she looked as if she had been crying. Dad, what have you done, she thought in frustration, leading the way around the greenhouse.

“What is it Charlene?” she asked patiently.

“Your father is seeing someone!” The admission came out in a trembling voice.

“Charlene, I am sure I am not the one to talk to about this. Why don’t you ask him?” she suggested.

“He said he wanted space.” She was twisting her hands together and her eyes were leaking.

“I see.” She had not spoken to either of her parents in several days and she realized that that was very unusual. Her father had called her and said that he was going out of town so he could not make their usual lunch date but she had been happy about it because she had been with David. “Look Charlene, he is my dad and I love him very much, but I am afraid he is not the most faithful person. You should know that because he cheated on my mom with you, remember?”

The girl sat down heavily on a green lawn chair in the room and she looked so desolate that Janice almost felt sorry for her. “I thought he was different from all the other losers I went out with.” She looked down at her clasped hands. “When he asked me to marry him, it was the happiest moment of my life and I thought: finally, someone who wanted more than just my body. I fell in love with him and I thought that he would fall in love with me as soon as we get married and settle down. Now I don’t know what to do. He is not taking my calls, and I go to his apartment and he is not there. I am asking you to speak to him for me please.”

Janice sighed and wished her parents would sort themselves out and not let her be caught in the middle of this mess. “I will try.” The girl looked up at her eagerly and Janice felt sorry for her. “I am not promising you anything, Charlene, because if he does not love you then there is nothing you can do to make that happen."

She stood up and straightened her shoulders, her large breasts printing out against her floral blouse. "I will accept that if he is man enough to tell me to my face." With that she left.

*****

She called her mother as soon as the coast was clear.

"Darling, I have not seen you in a while! Where have you been?" Janet asked her.

"Mom, Charlene was just here," she said interrupting the chatter.

"Who?"

"The woman Dad is engaged to. She just left, Mom, and she is a mess, saying that Dad told her he wanted space." She paused and took a deep fortifying breath. "You don't happen to know anything about that by any chance, do you?"

"That woman is stalking your father," Janet said firmly. "She has been calling his phone nonstop and is staked out at his apartment, the poor man is going out of his mind with the stress of it."

"That poor man is the one who got himself into this, Mom, and I would appreciate it if he would tell her that it is over. I don't want her coming to my place of work again, Mom," Janice told her in an irritated voice.

"I will tell him when he gets back from out of town," she said.

"So he is really out of town?"

"Of course darling," her mother said reproachfully. "You know your father would never break his lunch date with you for anything less than that."

"Tell him to sort it out, Mom. I don't like being put in this position."

"Okay darling, I will. Love you lots honey."

*****

He took her to a small secluded restaurant on the edge of town. He was greeted warmly by the Maitre D and they were shown to a table at the back of the room. She had gone home and changed into a simple black wool dress that wrapped around her and tied at the back. The neckline was plunging and revealed a hint of her generous breasts. She had used the flat iron to straighten her shoulder length hair and it drifted to her shoulders in gentle curls. “So what are we having?” she asked him brightly. Whenever they were together, he did not contribute much to the conversation and even though she had told him personal things about herself and her family, he never revealed anything and he never spoke about his wife. But she was patient and she was in love with him and could wait him out. He suggested the red snapper with zucchini and black olive tapenade.

“So how was your day?” she asked him softly. She loved the way the red shirt and dark blue jacket with red stripes looked on him. His hair was ruthlessly combed back from his forehead and she could not wait to mess it up.

He smiled at her faintly. “What are you doing?”

“Making conversation like a normal couple,” she told him with a smile.

“Why are you – I mean what if I can’t –“ he left the sentence hanging. Their entrée of clear pumpkin soup had arrived by then and they started drinking.

“What if you don’t love me back?” she asked him teasingly.

He stared at her for a moment but he did not answer.

She pushed aside the soup and leaned towards him. His eyes went to her cleavage and he felt his body tighten.”There is no fear of that happening. How do I know? Because you are already falling in love with me.”

“How do you know that?” he asked her huskily, his meal forgotten.

“You can’t do without me and you are always thinking about me,” she told him saucily

“I think about you a lot,” he agreed, his voice hoarse. He wanted her so bad that he was not very comfortable. She leaned in and kissed his lips slowly, pushing her tongue inside his mouth. He moaned and the kiss deepened his heartbeat quickening. He broke away from her, his breathing harsh when he heard the footsteps coming their way. He had never displayed his emotions in public before and he had to fight to control the urge to pull her out of her chair and devour her right there. What the hell was happening to him?

She gave him a soft knowing smile as she settled back to enjoy her meal. He looked at her in consideration all through the meal and he found himself laughing at something she told him. Janice reached out to take his hand that was resting on the table and squeezed it gently. With a slight hesitation, he turned his hand over and enveloped hers, his eyes meeting hers.

Chapter 7

“Are you seeing someone?” his mother asked him curiously. They were having dinner in the large formal dining room. It was Sunday afternoon and he kept glancing at the clock. He had been mysteriously unavailable for the past few weeks and she had noticed him coming home one or two nights very late but she had assumed he was working. He had told her that a new shipment of vehicles had come in and he was having them assessed.

“I think I am,” he said with a confused smile. She had also noticed that he did not look as sad as he had been before and there was a light in his dark eyes.

“You think or you know?” his mother asked him in amusement.

“I am seeing someone, but I don’t know what to think,” he gave an eloquent shrug. “She says she is in love with me and refuses to take no for an answer.”

“I would love to meet her,” Julia said softly, her heart picking up the pace.

“I am not ready yet,” he said with a shake of his head. “She has broken through the shield I put up and no matter how much I tell myself that I am not seeing her again, it does not work out quite like that.”

“Sounds like quite a woman,” his mother said hiding a smile. He was falling in love with her and he did not even know it.

Just then his phone rang and he glanced at the caller id, his expression changing. “Excuse me, Mother, I have to take this,” he said pushing back his chair and standing.

“Tell her hello for me,” she said with a smile.

He stared at her for a minute as if wondering how she knew it was Janice then hurried into the next room.

“I have strawberries and whipped cream and I am totally naked. Tell me you are on your way over.”

He thought he had gotten over how totally unpredictable she was but she always proved him wrong.

“Janice,” he groaned.

“Are you on your way?”

“I will be right there,” he told her breathlessly.

“Good because the whipped cream I rubbed on my nipples are melting and I need you to suck it off,” she told him blithely.

His breath was trapped inside his throat and his penis hardened painfully. “Don’t start without me,” he told her hoarsely.

*****

“If I had died on my way here, it would have been your fault,” he told her wryly. His heart had almost failed him as she opened the door completely naked and just stood there with whipped cream on her nipples and her pubic area. He had kicked the door shut behind him and started feasting on her. They had not made it to the bedroom, but he had pulled her down to the floor and made passionate love to her right there on the floor.

“I accept all responsibility for that.” They were in her bedroom on the bed and she was trailing her fingers down his naked torso causing a shudder to go through his body. It was unbelievable the effect she had on him. “So what do you want to do now?”

“I am sure you are going to tell me what we will be doing,” he told her dryly, capturing her hand as it ventured closer to his pubic area.

“It’s a nice day out so I think we should go take a walk in the park and feed the ducks in the pond.” She pulled her hand away and reached for his semi erect penis. “But later, much later,” She murmured, sliding her hand up and down his shaft.

“Anything you want,” he told her hoarsely, pulling her on top of him.

*****

“Our daughter is going to have your head,” Janet told him mildly as he took off his jacket and hung it on the coat hanger just inside the doorway. It had been drizzling and his closely shaved head was glistening with water. He had not bothered to go to his apartment but had come straight to the house. “Charlene went to see her and wanted to know if you were seeing someone.”

“Oh damn,” Richard said with a groan. “I am going to have to call her.”

“Who?”

“Janice, of course,” he told her. He had brought her back something, an antique ring dated back to the fifteenth century with a unique emerald in the middle. He knew how much she loved collecting antiques and he had thought of her when he had seen it. He had been doing a lot of thinking about them while he had been alone in his hotel room and he knew he wanted her back.

“What about Charlene?” Janet passed him a steaming cup of herbal tea with honey just the way he liked it. It was late Monday afternoon and he was planning to spend the night.

“I suppose I will have to deal with her,” he sighed. “Want to be with me when I talk to her?’ he asked her half jokingly.

“Not a chance. You made the mess, you are going to have to clean it up.” With that she went into the kitchen to prepare something for them to eat.

*****

She took his hand. He had resisted at first and then he relented. It was a beautiful day and being the second week of

May it meant that summer was rapidly approaching but the weather was still cool and there was a slight breeze. Families were out in their numbers and they saw a blanket spread out underneath the shelter of an old oak tree and a family of four enjoying their meal. “We should have packed a meal,” she said softly as she watched as the little girl with the blonde pigtails devoured her hotdog.

“We ate just before we left the house,” he reminded her. They had wandered over to the lake and she reached inside the bag she had carried and took out slices of bread, passing one to him. He stared at it as if he had no idea what to do with it.

“You use it to feed the ducks,” she indicated the birds swimming around. They sat there and fed them in silence for awhile and then she spoke. “I want children,” she murmured. He went still and felt something squeezing his heart. What was she talking about?

“I think we should go.” He made as if to stand and she held onto him tightly.

“I am not saying that I want children right now, David, relax. I was thinking after we got married and maybe a year or two down the road we could try." She was trying not to laugh at his hunted expression.

"You are assuming a lot," he told her grimly. "I did not tell you that I wanted to get married again let alone have children."

"I said eventually." She turned and faced him. "I am in love with you David, and I know you are shying away from the topic and maybe you do not want to believe it. But I am and it is not going to change."

"Eileen told me she loved me and I treated her love like something disposable." He gripped her hands with his none too gently. "I am not going to take the risk of that happening again. I think we should give each other some space."

Janice could have kicked herself for bringing up the word marriage; it was too soon for him.

"I don't need space and neither do you," she told him firmly. "Loving you is my responsibility and I am prepared to deal with it but I refuse to be shoved aside because you cannot deal with your emotions and your guilt. I am not your departed wife, I know what I am getting into and I am quite okay with it."

He stared at her for a moment as if not quite knowing what to make of her. "I cannot promise you anything," he said finally.

"I know what I am facing David, I am a big girl. Speaking of which, I want to feel you inside me and your lips on my nipples, so let's go home." She took his hand and pulled him up and then standing in front of him she looped her hands around his neck, bringing down his head to take his lips with hers. He took her mouth hungrily, his tongue delving inside and his body growing hard with desire. He tightened his arms around her and deepened the kiss forgetting where they were. It was she who pulled away, using her teeth to nip at his bottom lip causing a dart to zip through his body at an alarming rate. "Do you still need space?" she asked him huskily.

"No." His body was shaking against hers and he could hardly stand still. "No." He took her lips again and this time he had to forcibly put her away from him. They barely made it to the car parked a few feet away and he drove quickly to a secluded area where he dragged her over to his side and took out his painfully erect penis, burying it inside her straight to the hilt. As he moved within her, he held her face between his hands and plundered her mouth with his helplessly, his desire like a raging storm inside him. What he felt for her was so all consuming that he found himself pounding inside her, his hands roaming her body restlessly from the force of his passion!

*****

“I don’t want to talk about it right now, Lance.” Leah sank down on the side of the bed and eased her tired and aching feet out of her clogs. She had done a double shift at the hospital again and she had just come home, only to find Lance waiting for her, spoiling for a fight. He had been that way since she had gone out with the girls’ accusing her of cheating on him.

“Well tough,” he said coldly. “We have decided to give our marriage a try and I am the only one dong the trying. What is going on here, Leah?” He was a tall and handsome dark skinned man with close shaven head and a bulky frame. He had taken up working out at the gym and had become obsessive about it.

“I am on early tomorrow morning so I would love to get some sleep and I would appreciate it if you would let me.” She stood up and made her way to the bathroom.

“Don’t you walk away from me.” He pulled her back against him, his hands punishing.

“Let go of me,” she told him softly, suddenly remembering why she had decided to leave him in the first place. He had a jealous streak that was a mile long and had become so possessive that she had not been allowed to talk to any male at the hospital. “And I would like you to leave right now.”

“I am not going anywhere,” his tone was sinister and with a sudden movement he backhanded her across the cheek causing her to fly across the room. She laid there stunned, her ears ringing and for a moment she could not get up. Then she did, shaking her head to clear her ear of the ringing, and picking up a heavy glass vase, she held it aloft.

“I want you to leave right now before I forget I am into healing people and hit you with this.” The side of her mouth was bleeding and she was trying hard not to cry, she was not going to allow him to see any weakness. “I want you to stay away from me from now on and I will make arrangements for us to have different shifts. Please leave before I change my mind and call the cops.”

He made as if to come closer, but she lifted the vase, her intentions clear. With a careless shrug he left. Leah quickly went and locked the door behind him, securing the chain after remembering that he had a spare set of keys. Realizing that she had the vase in her hands she carefully put it on the table and slid to the floor, her head buried in her lap.

After she had calmed down sufficiently, she called her best friends.

*****

"Why didn't you call the police?" Candace demanded. She was fit to be tied. Both she and Janice had come over at once. Janice had had plans to be with David for the night but when Leah had called her she had quickly shelved them and told David she would see him tomorrow. He had hesitated and she had the feeling he had wanted to ask her why, but he did not know how to.

She held the ice against her friend's swollen lips and felt a spark of anger invaded her body. "Was this the first time?"

Leah nodded. "He was always possessive but he never went that far." It was painful to talk and she winced slightly. She could not believe he had hit her. She was in a field where she had seen many battered women and had secretly wondered why they put up with it and now it had happened to her by a man who had professed his undying love for her! How messed up is that?

“Are you going to do something about it?” Candace was so angry that she could not stay still.

“Candace, you are not helping,” Janice warned her. “I know you are upset and want to go and tear him from limb to limb, but we have to think about Leah first.”

“She is right.” Leah took the ice pack from Janice and placed it on the table. It did not hurt as much as before and her headache had drifted to a dull ache. “I need to do something about it. I am going to file a report at the station and I am going to press charges.”

“Are you sure about this?” Janice asked, holding up her hands as her friends looked at her quizzically. “I know. But considering that this is going to affect the rest of his life.“ She stopped suddenly. “What am I saying? Go ahead and do it, the bastard deserves everything he gets.”

*****

They went with her to file the report and she took out a restraining order against him. She was asked if she wanted to press charges but decided against it, saying the restraining order will do. He had tried calling her, but she had ignored the call. When he called again, Candace had answered. “Listen you poor excuse for a man, if you come near her again I am personally going to cut out your balls and feed them to some ducks I saw in the pond at the park. You got that?” She punched the off button and threw the phone on the bed, turning to find her friends staring at her in amazement. “What?”

They burst out laughing and that served to lighten the mood.

They spent the night with her and the three friends slept in the same bed and in the morning Leah called in sick and went to stay at Candace’s place for the day. “In case he gets any idea that he can come by while you are alone,” she said grimly.

*****

"You look like you did not sleep last night," Maggie commented as soon as she dragged herself to the store the next morning.

"Friend crisis," she said briefly, shrugging out of her light jacket. It had started to warm up and for the first week of June which was next week, they had a huge wedding to make arrangements for.

"The bride to be called just now and wants to change the order to daffodils and tulips instead of the peonies and baby's breath," Maggie told her. "You okay?" she asked in concern.

"I am just tired, Maggie," she said forcing a smile. "We have an order for some gladiolas and Lilacs for the tea party over at the community center. Do you think you can take Jake with you to set up?"

"Of course," Maggie said immediately. "I will go and make the arrangements."

She called her friend when she got a chance. "How are you?"

"Feeling like the biggest fool there is," Leah sad ruefully.

“You cannot blame yourself Leah, it’s all on him,” Janice told her firmly.

“What does it say for my taste in men Jan?” she asked wearily. “I was thinking of actually going back to him and I knew that something was off, he was too possessive and I ignored that. Why? Was it because I did not want to be alone?”

“Honey you have to stop beating yourself up. Just know that you are not going to allow it to happen again.”

“You got that right. I am going in to work tomorrow and I am going to be up front with my supervisor and I am not going to hide away from him and stay huddled into a corner. There is a support group at the hospital that I think I might just go to.”

“Good for you honey, talk to you later.”

She was just resting her head back against the chair when she heard the chime of the bell above the door. She heard when Maggie told the person that she was around the back and wondered who it could be when she saw him loomed in the doorway of her small office. He looked so handsome with his wind tousled hair and his expertly cut charcoal grey jacket suit and red shirt that she just wanted to jump into his arms and devour him.

“Hi,” she said huskily, watching him standing there.

“I tried calling you, but I got your voicemail. You okay?” he asked her in that irritatingly polite voice of his.

“I am now,” she told him softly. “You missed me!” Her expression was teasing and she saw with amusement as he looked around as if wanting somewhere to hide.

“I just wanted to make sure you were okay that’s all,” he told her stiffly.

“Is it so hard to say it?”

“Janice stop it,” he said tightly. “I have a meeting to go to so I guess I will see you later if you are not too busy.”

“Do you really have a meeting or is that just an excuse for you to run?” She had moved from around her desk and came towards him. “I missed you last night, but one of my friends had an emergency.” She looped her hands around his neck.

“You don’t owe me any explanation,” he muttered his hands still at his sides.

“I know I don’t, but you are my man and I want to explain.” She hid a smile at his panicked look at her mention of him as her man.

“I am not- I am-“ He stuttered to a stop as if not knowing what to say.

“You are trying to say you are not my man?” she asked him mildly. “I beg to differ.” Her hand went between his legs and she pulled down his zipper and took out his rising penis. “You are my man, make no mistake about that.” She gripped him in her hand and touched the tip of him.

“Janice, you need to stop.” His breathing had accelerated and he leaned back against the door jamb weakly.

“Tell me what I want to hear,” she whispered. “I missed you inside me last night and I was thinking about you. Tell me what you were thinking.”

“I was thinking about you,” he rasped, the words dragged from him. He gripped her arms and brought her closer to him. “I can’t do this here.”

“I know.” She released him and wrapping her arms around his neck, she took his mouth hungrily with hers while he closed his arms around her, crushing her against him, his mouth plundering hers.

It was the sound of laughter in the store that pulled them apart. He stood there staring at her his eyes unreadable and his jaws taut with the effort it took for him to control himself. He was a mess where she was concerned and he was not able to control himself around her. “I will come over later.” He zipped up his pants and closed his jacket over it and left without another word.

Janice forced the trembling to stop, by taking deep breaths. She had to go out to the store and she had to find some semblance of control first before she did so. With a confident smile on her full lips swollen by his kisses she knew he was more than half in love with her!

Chapter 8

The wedding happened on a very beautiful day. It was the first Sunday in June and the sun was brilliant in the clear blue sky. It had rained the night before and the rain drops were still on the plants and the colors of the flowers added a beautiful backdrop to the stark white of the chapel. She and her staff of two had been invited as guests as well and they had arrived earlier in the morning to place the floral arrangements on the inside of the church and had put garlands on the benches.

The ceremony was set to commence at one in the afternoon and Janice had gone home to get ready. She had asked David to attend with her and he had told her no and that had caused an argument.

“Why not?” she had demanded. He had been over the house on Saturday and she had told him about it after they had made love.

“I don’t go to weddings,” he had told her stiffly, climbing off the bed and pulling on his t-shirt. His hair was tousled from the movement of her fingers running through it.

“I would like you to go with me David as my date,” she said stubbornly, getting up and coming to stand before him completely naked. He had avoided looking at her because he knew he would weaken if he did and he was tired of losing control to her.

“Take your friends with you and I am sure you are not short of men who would be falling over themselves to take you,” he told her cruelly.

“You want me to invite some other man to take me the wedding?” she looked at him incredulously.

“We are not exclusive Janice, so you can do whatever you want,” he said, turning away from her.

“Are you seeing someone else?” she had asked him quietly.

“What?” He turned to look at her then.

“You heard the question David, so answer it.”

“I am not but maybe you should be, I cannot give you what you want.”

She stood there looking at him in silence, and for the first time since she had been with him she wondered if he was right. She had been trying and he was not even giving her the courtesy of meeting her part way.

“Maybe you are right,” she forced herself to say coolly and was intensely satisfied to see his look of confusion. She had thrown him for a curve and he had not expected it.

“Well yes.” He turned away to put on the rest of the clothes. “I hope you have a very enjoyable time.”

“One thing before you leave,” she told him.

“What is it?” His expression was unreadable and she could just feel him hiding his emotions.

She went up to him and unbuckled his belt and unzipped his pants.

“What are you doing?” he asked in panic.

“Something to remember me by,” she murmured and went down on her knees in front of him. She took out his penis and closed her mouth over it, her tongue swirling around the tip of it. She felt his body shudder and his breath hitched. She pulled him inside her mouth, her head moving up and down his shaft, her saliva leaving marks on him. His body moved as she increased the pace of her mouth and he felt as if he was going to burst. He tried to get her to stop for him to enter her vaginally, but she would not stop and instead used one of her hands to squeeze his testicles gently. That was what did it for him! With a hoarse cry, he emptied himself inside her mouth, his body bucking uncontrollably, his cries echoing inside the room! She swallowed him and kept swallowing until she had licked him clean, her tongue lingering on the tip of him and it was only then that she stood up.

He stared at her wordlessly, his body still shaking and weak. She put her hands around his neck and took his lips with hers, plunging her tongue inside his mouth, her hands sifting through his dark hair.

She pulled out of his arms suddenly. “Goodbye David, I have to go and find a date to attend the wedding.”

He stood there staring at her as if he could not believe she had just said that.

With a nod, he turned on his heels and left. Janice sank down on the bed, her body trembling. She had hated to do that, but she felt it was time she took a stand where he was concerned or he was going to continue taking her love for granted.

She reached for her phone. “Dad, I need a date for a wedding tomorrow.”

“Of course, darling. What time and where?”

*****

David paced the length of his home office, his brows furrowed and his hands clenched. He had woken up this morning with a splitting headache because he had not slept for most of the night. He was the one who told her that she should find someone else to take to the wedding and that they were not exclusive, so why was he feeling like crap and why did the jealousy inside him was threatening to consume him? He had tried to get her off his mind by getting some work done but that had not worked.

He had not eaten because he did not feel like eating and was sitting at his desk staring at nothing in particular.

There was a soft knock on the door and his mother came in bearing a tray with coffee and toast and orange juice. He stared at the clock and realized that it was almost nine-thirty. "I did not see you come down so I was wondering if you were okay."

"Thanks, Mother, I just did not feel hungry," he said, getting up and coming around to take the tray from her.

"Want to talk about it?" she asked him casually, taking a seat in front of his desk.

He hesitated a moment and then with a sigh he sat back down. "She asked me to attend a wedding with her and I told her to get someone else to take her."

"Oh David." His mother shook her head. "How do you feel about her?"

"I don't know." He tunneled his fingers through his dark hair. "She confuses me and when she told me that she was going to find someone to take her, I wanted to forbid her to do so. I don't know what is happening to me, I cannot think straight when I am around her."

Julia hid a smile; her poor son. "You don't think you might be falling in love with her?"

David stared at her, a frown on his brow. “I can’t fall in love with her, Mother. She was talking about marriage and children and I wanted to run, I am not ready for that yet.”

“The signs are all there, David,” Julia told him soberly. “How do you feel when you are not with her?”

“I miss her,” he said without hesitation. “I did not sleep very well last night.”

“There you go.” His mother said to him. “I think you might be in love.”

*****

“Not that I am not happy to be escorting such a beautiful woman to a wedding of all places, but how is it my very beautiful daughter does not have a date for the occasion?” Richard Langley asked his daughter as soon as he pulled up outside the church. She had driven her own car, knowing that her father probably had somewhere to be right after and she was planning to go and visit with Leah and Candace as soon as she left the church.

“My date stood me up,” she told him lightly, automatically adjusting his black bow tie as he leaned in to kiss her cheek. She was wearing a figure hugging floral dress and her hair was caught up in a neat chignon at the nape of her neck. The dress had a plunging neckline and she had put on a silver chain with a diamond pendant that nestled between her generous breasts

“Is he an idiot?” her father demanded, pulling her hand in his arm as they made their way inside. “Want me to straighten him out for you?”

“That’s sweet, Dad,” she told him dryly. “But considering that you are not able to straighten out your own life then I would have to say absolutely not.”

“Ouch baby girl, that hurts a little bit,” he told her with an irrepressible smile.

“How is everything with Charlene anyway?” she asked him. They made their way to a seat at the back. The church had filed up with people and she could see Maggie sitting beside her husband and Jake had a date in tow.

“I told her I wanted to talk to her and she has been avoiding me,” he muttered in an undertone.

“Do you blame her?”

“Not at all,” he said with a shake of his head. “I am in a very confused state of mind myself. I want to ask your mother to marry me again because I find that I am still in love with her and yet I have the feeling that she has gotten used to her freedom and does not want that anymore.”

“How the tables have turned,” she told him teasingly, reaching over to squeeze his hand. “We are quite a pair, aren’t we? I am in love with a man who is so eaten up with guilt about not loving his dead wife and you are in love with a woman you left for a woman you cannot stand now.”

“You are with someone?” He looked at her sharply. “How come we have not met him to find out if he is good enough to be dating our little girl?”

“I am a big girl now, Dad,” she told him dryly. “And you have not met him for the very reason that the relationship is tentative and I am giving it time.”

“Who is he?”

“I am not telling you yet until we sort ourselves out,” she told him firmly. “Now let’s enjoy the ceremony,” she told him, standing as the wedding march came on and the bride made her appearance.

“We are not finished,” he warned her.

*****

“How are you?” Janice asked as soon as Leah opened the door. The swelling had gone down and she almost looked like her old self again. She had come straight there from the wedding which had finished at a quarter past three.

“Very well considering I saw Lance twice at work but he never approached me.” Leah led the way into the cozy kitchen where she and Candace were preparing the simple meal of curried shrimp and salad and mashed potatoes. Candace waved at her as she sliced tomatoes for the salad. “He has been calling my phone but I am not taking his calls.”

“I told her to change her number,” Candace spoke up.

“I am not going to change my number,” Leah said firmly as she opened the bottle of wine and poured the red wine into three glasses, passing one to each girl. “I am not upending my life for a man.”

“How was the wedding?” Candace asked Janice, admiring the simple stylish dress she had on.

“Lovely. The bride was truly beautiful. I went with my dad,” she said, sipping her wine.

“I thought you were going with David,” Leah said looking at her quizzically.

“He told me to take someone else,” she said with a grimace. “But don’t worry, I have a plan to make him realize that there was no way he can be without me, you just wait.”

*****

She was not answering her phone and he knew she was doing it deliberately. But what if she wasn’t, a little voice inside his head asked him. What if she was actually with someone else? She had called him her man and he had felt a quiver go through him at the words. He could not concentrate on what he was doing. He was supposed to be checking the new shipment coming in and preparing some documents for a board meeting. He also had a meeting with the sales department to strategize on plans for the summer clearance sale but he could not get his head on straight. She had come into his life and turned it inside out. He glanced at the clock on his desk and saw that it was after five. He had been calling her since three o'clock, and she had not answered her phone.

With an impatient movement, he went into the bedroom and pulled on some clothes and headed out; he had to see her.

*****

Janice saw him on the porch when she got home. It was after six and she had told her friends that she was heading home. She had turned off her phone deliberately and when she turned it back on she had seen the number of missed calls from him. Good, she thought in satisfaction, now he would realize that he could not treat her as he wanted to and get away with it.

He stood up as she came up the steps. “Where were you?” His expression was furious.

“I was at the wedding I invited you to, remember?” she asked him mildly, opening the door with the keys she had fished out of your small clutch.

“I called you several times.” He came in behind her and slammed the door shut. “Who were you with?”

She turned to look at him and realized that his fists were clenched at his sides. “You were the one who told me to go with someone else, David. Don’t you remember?”

She almost relented when she saw the expression on his handsome face. He was wearing a white t-shirt and faded denims and he looked as sexy as hell! His hair was tousled and quite unlike his usual neat look and his face was etched in misery.

“Who was he?” he asked her softly, reaching out to pull her forcibly into his arms. “If you let him touch you-” he broke off and took her lips with his with bruising force, his arms tight around her.

Janice returned the kiss, her arms going around his neck. He picked her up and carried her into the bedroom where he laid her on the bed and knelt there looking down at her, his breathing labored. “What have you done to me?” he asked her achingly, peeling off her dress to reveal that she was not wearing a bra. He bent his head and started sucking her nipple, pulling it inside his mouth. Janice arched her body against his, her hands gripping his dark head.

He left her nipple and peeled off the dress and her blue silk panties, his hands wandering down her body. “Please tell me he did not touch you,” his voice was tortured and she knew she could not continue to let him suffer. She went on her elbows and captured his face in her hands.

“I went with my dad, baby,” she whispered. “I would never do that to you.”

With a whimper, he gathered her up against him and buried his head into her neck breathing in her exotic scent. Then he started kissing her all over her body, not stopping until he was thrusting inside her with his tongue, her cries echoing around the room as he brought her to an overwhelming release!

*****

He did not leave for the night. He spent the time exploring her body restlessly as if he could not get enough of her, he brought her to ecstasy over and over again and Janice was in a constant state of arousal, her skin flushed with heat.

"We need to talk," she told him. They had just finished making love for the third time and she was exhausted and still aroused and she could not believe it.

"Let's not." He took her lips with his softly, pushing his tongue inside her mouth. He was still inside her and she felt him moving within her. She tore her mouth away from his with firm resolve.

"David," she said gently, holding his face still with her hands.

"Don't ask me how I feel about you, Janice," he told her with a sigh. "I am in a state of confusion about what I am feeling. All I know is that I don't want to be without you and I cannot bear the thought of another man touching you," he said bleakly.

"That's a start," she told him gently. "Would you like something to eat?" she asked him, glancing at the clock. It was after midnight but she was starving.

"That's it?" He looked down at her.

“You were expecting more?” she asked him mildly, biting down gently on his bottom lip causing his body to shudder against hers.

“I was,” he informed her, capturing her lips with his in a brief kiss. “And yes, I would like something to eat.”

He came into the kitchen with her and watched as she deftly made huge turkey sandwiches and they ate them and drank some fruit juice from the bottle. He pulled her onto his lap and they ate like that completely naked with him nibbling at her neck in between. He spent the night wrapped up in her arms, his dark head buried between her breasts, his breath on her skin.

*****

“Who is this mystery man your father told me you were seeing?” her mother called her while she was at work on Monday. She was busy getting together some arrangements for a funeral that was happening that afternoon. Maggie had gone out with Jake to make some deliveries and the store had been busy since she had come in at eight. On top of that, she had not gotten enough sleep and her eyes were fighting to stay open. She had drunk gallons of coffee, but she was still not feeling energized. David had left at seven to go home to get ready to go to the office, but they had showered together and he had made love to her standing against the tiles, her legs wrapped around his waist and him thrusting inside her urgently. If they continued that way, they were going to kill each other.

“Hi Mom, and how are you? I am fine, by the way,” she said mockingly.

“Cut it out honey,” she said in irritation. “Your father told me you are in love with some guy who lost his wife or something like that. Is he someone suitable? How old is he by the way?”

“Mom, I am busy at work so I will talk to you later. David is twenty-seven years old and more than suitable,” she said, ready to end the conversation.

“Oh, so when are we going to meet him?”

“Not right now, Mom, and I already told that to dad.” She clipped off a dead leaf off the hydrangea and arranged it skillfully in the rest of the bouquet. “Love you, Mom, and bye.” She hung up before her mother could say anything else.

Her phone rang again as she was ringing up a customer. She looked at the caller ID and noticed that it was David. “Hi,” she answered softly.

“Hi,” he said quietly. “How are you?”

“Tired,” she admitted ruefully. The customer had gone and she was alone in the store at the moment.

“What do you want to do later?” he asked her.

Her eyebrows lifted. Usually she was the one asking him. “How about a movie?”

“Okay,” he paused. “You choose, I don’t much about movies.”

“No problem, I am an expert,” she told him with a laugh.

“I miss you,” he said suddenly. “I wanted to turn back when I was on my way to the office and be with you.”

Janice found herself trembling at his admission. It was the first time he had ever revealed his true feelings to her and she found it had a powerful effect on her.

“Oh David,” she breathed, her skin getting hot.

"I cannot wait to see you."

"Me neither," she murmured.

He hung up after that and she sat there with her heart beating hard and her skin hot to the touch. He had not said the words, but she knew he had fallen in love with her!

*****

David sat back in his chair, a smile curving his lips. He had told her and he had not felt as if it had been dragged from him. He missed her and he found that he wanted to be with her every single minute of the day. He did not know if it was love, but it was very close to it.

Chapter 9

Charlene made her plans carefully. At first she had thought about telling him that she was pregnant, but the time had already passed for that to be credible and besides he had always been careful to use a rubber. So that was out of the question. She had found out he had gone back to his ex-wife, the same woman he had told her he was never going back to. She was left feeling absolutely humiliated with people at the salon asking her when the wedding would be. She had always considered herself to be a good girl, she had even attended Sunday school when she was a child and had stuck to the rules most of the time. She remembered one time in her teenage years when she and some friends had gone to the mall to browse and they had snuck some make-up into their backpacks and had encouraged her to do so as well, but she had refused and had walked out of the store with her head held high. It did not matter that they had not hung out with her again; she had chosen honesty over shady friends and that had made her feel good.

She had gone out with a series of losers because she had been looking for a good man to settle down with and have children, but it had not happened until she had met Richard Langley. She had hesitated a little because he had been married at the time and she remembered her mother telling her that married men were curses straight from God and it would not do to be a home wrecker but she had consoled herself into thinking that the marriage was over before she had met him so she was not at fault. She had been led to believe that he was over his ex wife because the years had passed and she had gotten confident. Now she was stuck with an engagement ring and the man had gone back to his wife. He had called her and said he needed to talk to her, but she had not returned the calls, fearing the inevitable, and she had not gone back to his daughter as that had not turned out too well.

She was going straight to the source. She had followed him one night and found out where the wife lived and had stayed out there in the car shivering in the cold and with pain radiating through her broken heart after she had seen her wrapped in his arms before they closed the door. The bitch had stolen her man from her and she was going to pay for it!

*****

"I need to talk to you." Leah heard the voice behind her and spun around quickly. He was well behind her, but he was too near according to the restraining order.

"We have nothing to say to each other," she told him coldly. "And if you are not gone by the next minute, I am calling the cops."

"Please." He held up his hands. "I just want to say I am sorry about hitting you like that and I really don't know what came over me. I have not been the same since you left me, Lee, and I cannot function right now."

He looked a wreck and he had lost some weight, but even though she felt sorry for that, she was not going to fall for that again. She knew the drill: the self recriminations and the gifts and then before you knew it, the same thing happened again and she was not going to let him put his hands on her again. "You need help, Lance," she told him calmly. "You are going to have to get counseling. I cannot help you and I don't want to be with you anymore. What you did killed something inside me."

“Please don’t say that.” She could see the tears and it did not sway her one bit. “I love you Lee, and if I cannot have you then I don’t want to live.”

“You see Lance, that’s where you are wrong,” she told him gently. “I cannot be responsible for your happiness and you should not let someone have that kind of power over you. I am sorry.” She turned to leave and heard the sob that escaped him. She did not turn back to look at him but hurried inside the hospital, her peace of mind shattered!

*****

“When are you going to agree to marry me again?” Richard asked his ex-wife impatiently. July was making way for August and the heat had intensified with the coming of the month. The heat shimmered in the air and the air conditioners were on high alert. School was out and evidence of that was there as they wandered in front yards with water guns and inflatable pools to keep cool.

They were sitting on the front porch enjoying the evening sun and having tall glasses of lemonade and watermelons.

“When you sort out that mess with miss thing,” Janet told him mildly. She was not in a hurry to make it permanent again and was willing to bide her time. She had almost been destroyed when he left and she was not going to let that happen again.

“Why are you punishing me?” he asked her plaintively. He spent most of his time there and was thinking of giving up his apartment if she would only say the word.

“You think I am punishing you?” she asked him incredulously, sipping her iced liquid.

“I think you are because of the way I left.” He put his half-empty glass on the small table between them and turned to face her. “I was a fool and there is no fool like an old fool and I would like to make it up to you if you would let me.”

“You need to sort things out with that young lady first Richard, and then we go on from there,” she said firmly.

“I called her and left messages on her phone and she has not responded. Maybe she has forgotten all about me,” he said with a weak smile.

“Women don’t forget rejection, Richard. They plan a way at getting back to the person who rejects them,” she warned him.

“I am sure she is not planning anything,” he said soundly.

“I hope you are right.”

*****

She made him laugh and he realized that was what had been missing from his life: laughter. He had never been able to laugh around Eileen maybe because he had never loved her, but with Janice it came naturally. She would tell him stories from work or something about her parents and she would make it come out funny. She was also very impulsive. They would be having dinner at her place and she would suggest going to the park or to the inflatable pool she had around the back of the house. One night, they sat in the pool until about ten o’clock and he made love to her right there in the backyard for the neighbors to see and he did not care, he had never done something like that before.

She was clipping the sides and back of his hair for him. It was a balmy night and they were outside on the porch. And he had suggested it. "I promise I won't make you look like a freak," she teased him.

He had sat there and let her put scissors in his soft dark hair. He was used to a barber coming over to the manor and giving him a haircut twice a month and he was shocked that he was allowing her to do it for him.

"Okay, what do you prefer?" She had draped a towel around him and was standing behind him wielding a pair of scissors. "A crew cut or a Mohawk?"

"Janice." He twisted his head to look at her and saw the impish look on her exquisite face. She had come home from work and taken a shower and put on a tiny blouse that left her midriff bare and loose shorts that rode high on her thighs.

"Relax." She bent over and kissed him softly on the mouth. "I would never let my man go out looking like a total wreck."

"I should hope not," he retorted, his heart jumping at her reference to him as her man.

She talked while she clipped and was contented to carry on most of the conversation. She was quite used to his silences and realized he was talking more and more.

“There I am done.” She took away the towel and brushed the hairs from the back of his neck and then gave him a mirror to look at her handiwork. “What do you think?” she asked him a little anxiously.

“I think you could do this for a living,” he told her with a small smile.

“So you like it?” she asked, still not convinced.

“I like it.”

“Oh great!” She put away the scissors and jumped on his lap. “I should give you a haircut whenever you need one.”

“And deprive my barber of his livelihood?” he asked her mockingly, his arms coming around her and holding her close.

“Oh of course you have a barber,” she said with a grin. “Okay, maybe once in a while.”

"Why do you love me?" he asked her abruptly, his intense black eyes staring into hers.

She looked at him and realized that he was trying to make sense of what was happening between them. She trailed a finger around his mouth and lingered on the sensuous bottom lip and felt the shudder through his body. "I love you because I cannot help myself," she told him quietly. "I love you because you are intense and sexy and when you touch me I dissolve into tiny pieces. I love you, David Hattori, because you are the first man for me and you were the one I have been waiting for all my life. Does that break it down for you?"

He nodded, his throat clogged and he felt the moisture in his eyes. "I have never told you I loved you back," he whispered.

"I know you do, but you cannot bring yourself to say it yet," she told him gently. "You have been telling me with your body for some time now."

"Janice," he whispered brokenly, dragging her head down to meet his mouth, his lips claiming hers in a kiss that left them both shaken and trembling. She clung to him tightly, molding her body to his.

He lifted her and went with her to the bedroom. “I have never experienced anything like this before.” He knelt before her, his mouth drifting down to her bare torso, pulling the skin between his teeth and sucking on it. Janice cried out as the sharp dart of desire shot through her body. He eased off her shorts and his eyes narrowed when he discovered that she was not wearing panties. “You make me weak with want,” he told her huskily, parting the lips of her vagina he bent his head and licked between the folds tenderly. He was taking his time and she realized that his feelings for her had shifted and he was letting her know. She was shivering from the desire racing through her body and her hands clenched at her sides. “Let me show you how much,” he murmured deeply. He used his fingers inside her and touched his mouth to her mound, sucking the skin into his mouth while he moved his fingers inside her. Janice was sobbing! She could not help it. He was driving her crazy with intense need. She came against his mouth after only a short time, and he thrust his tongue inside her to lick her clean.

“David,” she sobbed out his name and reached for him.

“I am right here baby,” he said soothingly and climbed on top of her, releasing his erection and putting it inside her.

“I can’t.” She held him tight to her, her body swirling out of control. “I love you so much!” He captured her cries with his lips and started moving inside her.

“I know baby, I know,” he whispered against her mouth.

*****

She waited until they had gone inside before she made her move. She had seen them cozying up out on the porch sipping cold drinks and talking and laughing. Probably talking about me, she thought bitterly. Well she was going to get the last laugh, she thought grimly.

As soon as they went inside, she was galvanized into action. She crept from her car and looked around furtively to see if any nosy neighbors were on the lookout. She knew she was taking a big risk because it was summer and people tend to be outside and it did not get dark until sometimes after nine, so she had waited.

She took out the kerosene pan from the trunk and she made sure she had her lighter with her and crept towards the house. A very nice house, she thought sneeringly, as she spilled the oil all around the perimeter of the building. Something inside her whispered that it was not worth it, she was doing all this for a man and he was not worth it, but she wanted revenge. She had just struck the match at the front of the porch when she heard someone called out to her. “Hey, what are you doing?” She froze looking at the fire that was spreading at a rapid pace and when she heard the front door opened, she fled to her car. The person who had called out to her did not look at her but had run up towards the house, dragging out his phone to make a call. By this time, the entire house was surrounded by fire and the neighbors had started to come out with buckets of water to douse the flames. Charlene drove off with a squeal of tires and raced away, her heart hammering!

*****

The damage was minimal, thanks to the quick actions of the neighbor, Mr. Fearon, who told the police what he saw and described the woman to them. The flames had damaged the front porch and the garden, but other than that, everything was intact and the occupants were not hurt.

“I know who she is, Officer,” Richard Langley said quietly, not looking at his ex-wife, knowing that she was never going to say yes now.

"I see." The man gave him a knowing look. "Know where we can find her?"

Richard gave him the address, his heart heavy at what he had caused her to do and he shuddered to think what had almost happened.

"Is there somewhere you can stay for the night?" the officer asked them.

"I will stay at a hotel for the night," Janet told him, not even looking at Richard. She had warned him something like this was going to happen and he had not listened.

"And you, Sir?"

"I have an apartment," he said quietly.

*****

"Mom, why didn't you call me!" Janice exclaimed. She had been totally unaware of what had happened the night before and shivered as she remembered how David had kept her busy for most of the night.

"I did not want to scare you honey," Janet told her with a sigh. "That woman is a total psychopath. I understand the idiot went straight back to her apartment and that's where the police caught her. She confessed to everything."

"I know I should not sympathize with her after what she had done, but I really feel sorry for her," Janice murmured. She had not too long arrived at the store when her mother had called and told her the story.

"I don't," her mother told her staunchly. "You don't go burning someone else's house just because a man left you. No man is worth all that."

"Yes Mom, you and I might think that, but some people take rejection very different," Janice said, still feeling sorry for the girl. "Dad did not handle the situation very well so he is partly to be blamed."

"I am sure he is in his lonely apartment rethinking his life now," she said grimly.

"You two are not a thing anymore?"

“He needs to stew in his juice for a little bit and fix my front porch and replant my precious flowers and then maybe I will consider taking him back.”

“Mom you have become quite the ‘b’ word, haven’t you?” Janice said in amusement.

“Darn right I have,” she told her daughter with a laugh. “Now, on to more pleasant things. As soon as your father has redone the porch, I want to meet your young man and have him over for dinner.”

“I will see what I can do.”

*****

“Oh my Lord, what on earth is going on?” Candace asked, throwing up her hands in the air. They were having lunch at a nearby restaurant and Janice was telling them about what had nearly happened. “Thank heavens that neighbor was around to call out to her and preventing anything worse from happening.”

“I shudder to think what might have happened myself,” Janice said picking up the cold shrimp and popping it inside her mouth.

“So what’s going to happen to her now?” Leah asked.

“She is going to jail of course,” Janice said with a sigh. “I told mom that I feel sorry for her and she thinks I am crazy.”

“You are always feeling sorry for people,” Candace told her dryly. “You cannot allow your emotions to get the better of you and when it comes to men, then that’s the worst thing you could ever do.”

“You sound like a woman who has had it with men,” Leah said looking at her friend.

“I am,” she said with a shrug. “I can’t seem to find a good one.”

“I think I have found one,” Janice said with a slow smile.

“We know, your billionaire lover,” Candace said with a grin.

“Hmm,” she murmured. “He is one of a kind.”

*****

Lance stared at the gun in his hand and wondered if he was brave enough to use it. He had tried forgetting her, but he had not been able to do so. He had gone out with a nurse or two and had even taken one of the female doctors to bed, but it had not worked and he had ended up feeling empty and alone. It had to be Leah or no one else. He had watched her from afar to see if she was going out with anyone else, but so far she was alone, apart from being with her girlfriends, and he had been happy about that because he would have had to take matters into his own hands and dealt with the person she was seeing. He had hit her because he had felt the rage rise up inside him when she had disregarded him and he wished he could take it back. Why wouldn't she believe him when he told her it would never happen again? Why was she being so stubborn?

He fingered the .22, his hand, his mind drifting back to happier times when they had just gotten married and had worked double shifts at the hospital. They had come home together in the pouring rain and hurried into the tiny apartment and had made love, tearing off their wet clothes and sinking into each other, their cries echoing inside the apartment.

He had wanted to have children with her and grow old with her, but she had decided that she did not want him anymore because he was too possessive. Didn't she see that it was because he loved hr so much that was why he held on so tight? Some women would be happy to be getting all the attention from their man but not dear Leah. She was different!

*****

Richard Langley sipped the liquor disconsolately. He had to look at Charlene and hear her admit to torching his ex wife's place with the intention of killing them both and he felt totally responsible for her actions. If he had not asked her to marry him and then not bother to honor that promise, then it would not have happened. Now he was left alone in his apartment, his wife was not talking to him, and a formerly nice girl was in lock-up because of him. His daughter had told him that he had a lot to think about and he should take the time to do so. Women, he thought, taking a swallow of the liquid and grimacing. He wished sometimes he could do without them!

Chapter 10

He brought her a gift. She had told him what happened at her parents' place and he had sympathized with her. That night, when he came over, he brought her diamond earrings in a black velvet box and she had no doubt that they were real. When he had passed her the box when they were having dinner, her heart had skipped a beat, thinking that it was a ring but had forced her disappointment away when she opened the box and saw the earrings winking at her.

"Do you like them?" he asked her anxiously.

"Yes," she said with a dazzling smile, but she had not taken into account how intuitive he was and how he was coming to know her.

"I am not ready for that yet, Janice," he said quietly, putting aside his wine glass. He still shielded away from anything concerning marriage and commitment and although she knew he was into her and that he probably loved her, it was very frustrating for him not to tell her anything. She wanted more, she wanted to be his wife and bear his children and the waiting was wearing on her.

“I know, but that does not make it any better for me,” she told him with a sad smile. “I want more, David.”

He got up and went to the window. “You knew how I felt before you started this Janice, and I will not be railroaded into another marriage,” he said grimly.

“How dare you!” she hissed, pushing back her chair and facing him, her hands on her hips. “You think I would force you into marrying me? Who the hell do you think you are?”

“I am sorry-“ he began, but she did not allow him to continue.

“I love you and I have put up with your crap because I love you, David Hattori, and for you to say I am forcing you into marrying me, that’s the last straw. I would like you to leave.” Her heart quaked inside her, but she was determined to stay strong. He knew how she felt about him and if she continued like this, she was never going to get a commitment from him.

“What?” He looked at her in shock.

“I want you out of my apartment. You know where I live and I don’t know where you go when you leave here. I tell you everything about me and my family, but you never reveal anything about yourself. I am sick of this David, and I deserve more." She was fighting hard not to cry.

"You said you were willing to wait," he protested, his heart hammering inside his chest.

"How long David? A few months? Or even a year? How long?" she asked him.

He stared at her mute. "I don't know, can't we just continue as we are?" he pleaded.

"No," she told him in a quiet defeated tone. "I want more and until you are prepared to give me more, I don't want to see you again."

He stood there staring at her, not moving, not believing what she was saying to him. "You don't mean that," he whispered.

"David, go please." She folded her arms across her breasts. If he touched her even slightly, she was a goner.

He stood there as if uncertain what to do and Janice felt herself praying that he would tell her he cannot live without her, praying that he would say that he loved her and wanted to be with her all the time, but instead he just left and closed the door quietly behind him.

Janice went over to the window and watched him go into his vehicle. He sat there for a little bit staring out in front of him and even at that time she was hoping that he would come back inside and demand that she be with him but he drove away. She slid down to the ground and folded her head into her drawn up knees and then the tears came and would not stop!

*****

Richard had the porch redone, and he had hired a gardener to do the landscaping of the place. He was even planting some orange and pear trees because he had been told that the soil was good for them. He had ordered the flowers from his daughter's store and work was currently in progress. Janet had moved back in and she was still thinking about letting him back into her good graces, even though it had been three weeks. September had arrived with rain and biting cold, and she stood in front of the big bay window and watched as the men did the work in the garden.

It was Sunday afternoon and Janice had come over for dinner.

“When are you going to let him know you forgive him, Mom?” she asked quietly. They had finished eating and she was clearing away the dishes off the table.

“I think I am going to let him stew for a little bit more,” she said with a laugh. She moved away from the window and came to sit around the table. She had been looking at her daughter and she noticed how wan and thin she looked. It was not her usual laughing demeanor and she looked as if she had been crying.

“Sit darling,” she suggested. “Now, tell me what is going on with you.”

“Apart from the fact that summer is in the past and it is already getting cold?” she asked lightly.

“This is your mother, honey, so why don’t you tell me the truth.” Janet poured some coffee and handed her a cup and then one for herself.

“I broke up with David two weeks ago,” she said staring at the steam rising from the liquid.

“Why?” her mother asked her gently.

“He is not willing to commit and I am not standing for it anymore,” she smiled sadly. “I think the joke is on me, he has not called me in two weeks, so I guess I never really meant anything to him at all.”

“You don’t really believe that, do you?” Janet asked her softly.

“I don’t know what to think, Mom. All I know is that I miss him so much that I cannot stand the pain inside me. I never knew I could fall so hard for someone and the fact that I did and I here without him makes me wonder if it was all worth it.”

“You gave him an ultimatum, honey, and from what you have told me about him, it seems to me he is scared and as much as he probably wants to acknowledge what he feels for you, he is afraid to do so because of what happened in the past.”

“I love him, Mom, and I respect what he went through but I guess I underestimate how scared he is,” she said sadly. “I cannot call him and let him think that everything is okay and I am willing to accept anything. He has to want me as much as I want him.

*****

But he did! David hid behind mountains of work as he had done in the past to try and get away from his true feelings. He had piled on the work, pushing his staff more and more and going to look at the shipments himself when he had people to do that. He rarely went home and his mother had started to worry about him. Even on Sundays, he was at the office and he slept there sometimes. She cornered him one morning when he was rushing out at seven-thirty to go to the office.

She had gotten up very early and stood outside the doors of his suite waiting for him to come out.

“Mother, what are you doing out here?” he asked in surprise. He did not look well. His cheeks had sunken into a hole and he looked as if he had not bothered to shave.

“I wanted to have a word with you,” she told him, trying to hide her concern.

“Can’t this wait until later? I have something to take care of at the office,” he said impatiently.

“It cannot wait,” she said firmly, leading the way into his sitting room. “You look like hell,” she told him bluntly. “And I know it is not because of Eileen’s death because you never looked that way so I want to know what is happening with the girl you were going out with."

"We have stopped seeing each other," he said abruptly, remaining standing, with his briefcase in his hands. "It did not work out."

"Is that it David?" she asked him quietly. "Are you going to let her go like that without a fight?"

"She told me to go," he told her rigidly, his hands clenched. "I am respecting her wishes."

"Oh David," his mother cried softly. "What happened to you? You are clearly suffering because of not been with her and yet you are so caught up in whatever it is you are caught up in that you will not allow yourself to be happy. When are you going to stop punishing yourself?"

"I will see you later, Mother, I have to go," he told her stiffly and left.

Julia sat where she was, staring at the closed doors, her expression one of complete and utter sadness.

*****

He would not allow himself to think or feel. He was disciplined and in control and he used work to forget her but it worked up to a point. He drove himself throughout the day so that he would be very tired during the night and he would just go to sleep but it had not worked out that way. He was barely getting any sleep and he was always thinking about her. Sometimes he would wake up in the middle of the night and thought she was in the room because he smelled her perfume, but she was not there. He missed her so much that it was a constant ache inside his heart and he did not know how to make it stop. He thought that the guilt associated with not loving Eileen was the worst he had felt, but he had never accounted for this, it was something that he could not contend with.

She had told him she wanted total commitment or nothing at all, and he had been trying to come to terms with it. She had told him she would wait until he was ready and she had gone back on her word, leaving him aching and missing her so much that he could not function. Why hadn't she left him alone? To his horror he felt the tears slipping down his cheeks and he hurried inside the bathroom, slamming the door shut behind him and resting his head against the door he wept in despair!

*****

“Maybe you should reconsider,” Leah told her. It had already been three weeks since she had heard from David, and her raw pain had turned into a dull pain in her breasts. It was Monday night and they had met up at Leah’s place to just hang out. Leah had not seen Lance for two weeks now and found herself grateful that he had probably accepted that they were over.

“Reconsider what?” Janice asked her.

“You are miserable without him and you look as thin as a rake.” Leah sipped the homemade pina colada as she stared at her friend. Her face had been thrown into sharp relief, but instead of detracting from her looks, it only added to them.

“He has not called me either,” Janice said with a shrug.

“So you are punishing each other,” Candace commented.

“I am not punishing him, I am just taking a stand.” Janice sipped the alcohol laced fruit punch and wished it was a sedative to knock her out for days. She was not handling the break up well, and she was running out of options on how to deal with it.

“Your stand is obviously backfiring on you,” Leah told her gently. “You should at least try and talk to him.”

“I have to stick by what I said or else what I did would have been for nothing. I want marriage or nothing, no matter how much I love him.”

*****

Lance waited outside until he was sure they had settled in. He had stayed away from her deliberately over the past two weeks to let her think he had gotten over her and moved on. He had watched her from afar and had not seen her with anyone and he had been so relieved. Maybe she was not over him.

He was not able to function and he knew he could not live without her at all. He did not want to.

With a sudden decision, he exited the car, looking carefully at both sides of the road to see if there was anyone looking at him. The streets were deserted maybe due to the rain earlier, and he made his way into the apartment building. He nodded to a man coming out of apartment 1B and made his way up to hers. He still had his keys and he hoped she had forgotten to change the locks. He put the key inside and sagged with relief as it fit, and turning it carefully, he let himself inside. He heard them immediately as they laughed about something, probably about me, he thought bitterly, feeling the gun in his jacket pocket.

It was Janice who first noticed him standing just inside the doorway. She felt a quake of fear and then she straightened up. “We have a visitor,” she told her friends quietly. Both of them looked up at once and saw him there.

Leah jumped up immediately. “What are you doing here Lance?” she asked him, her heart thudding in fear.

“I need to talk to you,” he said barely giving her friends a glance. He looked haggard and his eyes looked wild.

“You are not supposed to be here,” Leah told him firmly, determined to show not one ounce of fear.

“I need to talk to you alone,” he insisted, coming further into the room.

“We are not leaving,” It was Candace who answered him.

“Stay out of this bitch!” he snarled.

“I am calling the police,” Leah said, reaching for the phone.

“I don’t think so,” he said calmly, taking out the gun and pointing it at them. “We are going to talk, Leah.”

“What are you doing?” Leah’s voice sounded strangled.

“I have tried to reason with you and you will not listen. I have told you we belong together and you have slighted me and ignored me. I bet you are listening now.”

“I am listening,” she said faintly.

Janice reached out and gripped Candace’s hand wishing frantically that she had not left her pocketbook so far away with her phone inside.

He pulled up a chair and waved them to sit back down. “One funny move and I am not afraid to use it,” he threatened. He started talking about how much fun they had had in the past and how he wanted that back, but she had taken it away from him and he could not function without her. “What did I ever do that was so wrong?" he asked her, his voice anguished. "You gave me your love and your body and cruelly took it away, what am I supposed to do?"

"I am sorry about that Lance," Leah told him quietly. "Maybe I could have handled it better, but I just knew that I was not prepared to live like that again. You had gotten too possessive and you never trusted me. Love cannot survive without trust."

"I want another chance." He waved the gun at them, causing them to jump back. "I am not leaving here without you."

"Okay, I will come with you, just let my friends go," she told him.

"No way," Candace said stoutly. "We are not letting you go with him."

"Shut up bitch!" he screamed, jumping up from the chair and using the side of the gun to smash it on Candace's face. She slumped to the ground unconscious, blood streaming from the side of her head.

Suddenly there was pandemonium! Leah screamed and as he turned towards her, Janice jumped on him without thinking, sinking her teeth into the soft flesh of his neck. With a furious scream, he flashed her away from him and fired off a shot in her direction. Leah used a vase on the table and smashed it hard on his head, and he slumped to the ground, out like a light!

*****

Janice felt herself going in and out of consciousness. She was aware of people talking around her and a blinding pain in her left arm.

Leah gripped her hand only letting go as they wheeled her into the emergency room. She had called her parents and they were on their way over. Candace had suffered a concussion and was awake now although the doctor had told her that the bullet had passed through Janice's arm, she had lost a lot of blood.

She could not believe this was happening. She had thought that both of her friends were dead and her training as a nurse had deserted her in that crucial moment. The police and ambulance had come immediately and Lance was also being treated then he would be processed and taken into custody. It was all her fault, and if there was any lasting damage to her friends, she would never forgive herself. She had thought it had all been over and never gave Lance a second thought.

Janice's parents rushed inside just then and saw the girl with tears on her cheeks. "Where is our daughter?" Janet asked her urgently.

"She is in surgery," Leah told her miserably. "I am so sorry, Mrs. Langley."

"For what?" Janet asked her impatiently. "Did you shoot her?"

"What did the doctor say?" Richard Langley asked before the girl could respond.

"The bullet went straight through, but she has lost a lot of blood."

"What happened?" he asked her grimly.

Leah told him about Lance and the restraining order she had taken out on him. "I thought he had moved on," she said sadly.

"They rarely do," Janet said quietly, looking at her ex-husband.

It was another hour before the doctor came forward. "How is she, Doctor?" Richard asked urgently.

"You are her father?" the elderly man asked him.

"Yes."

"She is going to be okay, the bullet went straight through and we have given her some blood for what she has lost. She is resting now but you can go in and take a peek at her." He turned to Leah. "Candace is asking for you."

*****

"How do you feel?" Leah gripped her friend's hands, her heart turning over as she saw the big white bandage on her forehead.

"Like I have been gun butted," she said weakly. "How did you and Janice get away?"

Leah bent her head and burst into tears.

"Hey," Candace said alarmed. "I am still here honey, and don't you go blaming yourself for what that creep did, it's all on him."

“He shot Janice,” Leah blurted out.

“Oh my Lord!” Candace exclaimed weakly. “Is she…” She could not continue.

“She just came out of surgery and the doctor said she is going to be okay,” Leah assured her.

“Oh thank goodness!” Candace slumped back weakly against the pillows. “How did you get out in one piece?”

“I smashed the vase on his head.”

“Good for you, honey,” Candace said approvingly.

“How did this happen Candace?” she asked her friend, her eyes filling up with tears again. “How did I not see it?”

“How could you?” Candace asked her gently, squeezing the hand holding hers. “He was crazy dressed up as normal, and I guess the crazy came out when you left him.”

“Did I make him do this?”

“He made him do it,” Candace told the girl firmly. “You are not responsible for his actions.”

*****

“What if we had lost her?” Janet asked softly looking at how still her daughter was. There was a bandage on her upper arm and she looked so peaceful.

“We have not lost her and we have to be thankful for that,” Richard said holding her hand inside his. “I want to go and find that son of a bitch and kill him with my bare hands.”

“Then we would be losing you.” Janet slipped her hand out of his and put it around his waist. “I could not bear that.”

He looked down at her and his expression softened. “I am moving back in and I want no argument from you. We have wasted too much time already and we are not going to waste anymore.”

“Okay, Sir,” she told him softly, reaching up to kiss him on the lips gently. “I would not have it any other way.”

Chapter 11

She woke up in the early hours of the next morning. It was a little dark in the room and she waited until her eyes had become accustomed to the darkness. She moved her left arm and cried out a little bit at the pain and then the memories came flooding back!

“Don’t move your arm,” a deep voice said softly and it was then she realized that David was in the room.

“David?” she whispered confused. “What are you doing here?”

He came and sat gingerly at the side of the bed. He looked as if he had not slept the night, his eyes were red and his hair was tousled and untidy. “Your mother found my number in your phone and called me.” His hands were trembling and he looked at her in abject misery. “I could have lost you and I was such a fool.”

“You were,” she teased him trying to lighten the mood. She used her right hand and took one of his. “I am here, David.”

"Ask me again." His hand tightened on hers. "Ask me again what I want."

"What do you want, David?" she asked him softly.

"I want to wake up in the mornings with you. I want to go to bed with you at nights and I want to make love to you over and over again until we both die of old age. I want to see my children growing inside you and I want us to get married, and I don't want to be apart from you for a single day. I love you Janice, and it took my almost losing you to know that."

Janice felt the tears clouding her eyes and she had to blink them away. "Then it was a good thing I got shot," she joked weakly.

"Don't say that!" he said sharply. He lifted her hand and kissed her palm causing the shiver to go through her body. "I want to find that son of a bitch and I want to strangle him with my bare hands. He hurt you and I cannot bear that. Janice baby, I almost lost you, I almost lost you!" To her shock, he started weeping, the tears coursing down his cheeks unchecked. She brought his head down against her and held him stroking his dark hair tenderly, amazed at the amount of emotions he was displaying.

He eased up off her. “I am sorry,” he muttered, getting ready to move away.

“Don’t!” she warned him. “You don’t get to do that again, David Hattori.”

“I won’t,” he promised quietly. “I love you Janice, more than you will ever know.”

*****

He did not leave her, even when the doctors and nurses came in to check her vitals and even when her parents were there and Leah and Candace came in, hugging one another and talking all at once. He stood there in the corner of the room as if he was standing guard over her. Jake and Maggie came by for a visit bringing flowers and updating her on what was happening at the store.

It was Tuesday afternoon and she could not believe that it was only yesterday that everything had happened.

“How are you?” she asked Leah quietly. Her friend looked haggard and riddled with guilt, and even though she and

Candace had told her that it was not her fault, she still had not accepted that.

“Hanging in there.” She looked over to where David was sitting doing something on his laptop. He had gone home briefly to shower and change and refused to go into work and leave her, so he had carried his work with him and stationed himself inside her room. “I did not see it coming Janice, I did not see how unstable he was and he almost–“ She broke off in abject misery looking down at her clasped hands. “I am sure everyone hates me, especially him,” she whispered looking towards David.

“David wants to strangle Lance, but he does not hate you.” She gripped her friend’s hands trying to transfer some reassurance to her and get her out of her funk. “Nobody saw it Leah, and you have to be thankful that it happened this way. It could have been you alone in that apartment and it could have gone another way.”

“You are right.” She took a deep breath and tried to smile. “Candace said my leaving him brought the crazy out.

“In her own Candace way, she is right,” Janice said with a smile. She glanced at the silent man in the corner of the room and her eyes softened with incredible love. “We cannot be responsible for someone else’s actions Leah, and we have to remember that.”

“So he has finally declared his love huh?” she whispered.

“He has. He asked me to marry him,” she said with a smile. “I said yes, of course.”

*****

She was released on Wednesday and he was the one who took her home. Her parents were behind them in their vehicle. Leah had gone to Candace’s apartment with her, where she would be spending a few days with her.

He lifted her up and took her inside placing her gently on the sofa. “You do realize that I was shot in my arm and not my leg, right?” she asked him teasingly.

Her parents came in just then. “If the man wants to spoil you let him,” her mother told her with a smile, easing up her daughter’s feet and placing them on the footstool.

“I agree.” Her father clapped David on the shoulder and kissed his daughter’s cheek gently. “We almost lost you darling, so we are determined to pamper you.”

“In that case, can I get all the money in your accounts?” she asked them sheepishly.

“You won’t need it,” David told her quietly, coming to kneel in front of her. “I am going to give you everything you ever wanted. There is nothing in this world that you want that I will not give to you.”

Her parents stood there looking down at the man kneeling in front of their daughter and felt the wonder and amazement at the love portrayed there.

“All I need is you,” Janice told him softly, reaching out with her uninjured hand to brush back the hair from his forehead. “I love you.”

“I love you too.” He captured her hand and placed it against his jaw, his eyes closed.

Richard and Janet quietly left knowing that they had been excluded and the couple did not even realize that they had left so wrapped up in each other they were.

*****

He took her home to meet his mother. Julia Hattori embraced her fondly and welcomed her to the manor.

“I should have known you lived in a mansion,” she teased him as he took on a tour of the place. “What you must have thought when you spent time in my place.”

“I loved your place because you are there,” he told her simply. They were in his suite of rooms and she was sitting on his huge king-sized bed while he changed out of his street clothes and put on a sweat pants and a t-shirt. He had gone into the office for a couple of hours but not before he knew she had someone there with her. It was Friday afternoon and apart from going into the store for a short time, she was staying at home and recuperating. She was still wearing a sling, but her arm was getting better.

“How about a December wedding?” He had come up on the dais and was kneeling in front of her.

“You think we can plan a wedding in two months?” she asked him, her well-shaped brows rising.

“I will hire a wedding planner and take away the trouble of the planning from you,” he insisted.

She pushed away the hair from his forehead and met his intense dark eyes. “I want us to be honest with each other. Why do you want to marry me?”

He looked at her in surprise. “I want to marry you because I love you and I cannot see my life without you. I let my pride and my guilt got in the way before and I almost lost you. I never loved Eileen, baby, and I have come to grips that it did not matter if she was still alive, I would not love her still. I love you and you are the only one I want and it’s as simple as that.”

“In that case, a December wedding it is,” she told him with a catch in her throat leaning down to capture his lips with hers.

“Janice, your arm,” he protested.

“I need you,” she told him huskily, tightening her hand around his neck. “Now please, it’s been too long.”

“I don’t want to hurt you,” he said hoarsely, standing up and carefully putting her to lie on the bed. She was wearing denims and a short thick sweater and he carefully undressed her lingering over the lace underwear she was wearing before taking them off. He undressed before joining her on the bed, passing his hands over her naked body. He bent his head and flicked his tongue over her nipple causing her to arch her body towards his. He drifted down to her pubic area and dipped his fingers inside her slowly at first and then eagerly. He took her lips with his tenderly, his tongue entering her mouth slowly as his fingers thrust inside her. Janice felt the fire burning inside her and she wanted more, she wanted him so much that she found it hard to stay still.

His kisses were slow and drugging, infusing her body with warmth and she felt it down to the very core of her. It was as if he was trying to transfer his very soul to her and she felt herself molding to him, her body one with his, their hearts beating at the same tune. He took his fingers out and slide on top of her, careful not to touch her left arm. He entered her slowly, suspended over her and not moving as he gazed down at her, his dark eyes turbulent. “Let me show you how much I love you,” he murmured. He started moving inside her and as she wrapped her legs around him, her arms tight around his neck, her body lifting and moving against his.

Making sure he was not touching her injured arm, he thrust inside her urgently, the buildup of feeling inside him. He felt as if he was bursting with need for her and he knew he was not going to last long. He pulled out of her slightly and she murmured, moving restlessly against him. “Hush baby,” he muttered, entering her again, his eyes closed and his teeth gritted as her tightness closed around him. She pulled his head down to hers and claimed her lips with his as she felt the sensation rising from the bottom of belly straight up and she stiffened and went rigid as the orgasm rushed through her like a tunneling wave! He came with her, his thrusts becoming more urgent and the force so frantic that he felt as if he was falling from a cliff! He could not believe that such feeling was possible and he tore his mouth away from hers and cried out, his throat hoarse and parched with the need of her. His body shuddered against hers, and she held him against her trembling and spilling his seed inside her as if he would never stop!

He wanted to move off her, but he could not move. “Am I hurting you?” he asked her huskily, resting his head on hers, his breathing raspy.

“No.” She ran her hand down his back slowly, still feeling the shudder of his body against hers. “I want you to stay this way for a while.”

“If I do I am going to make love to you again,” he told her huskily. “I really think I should make you rest.”

“We have not seen each other for three weeks, and during that time I got shot in the arm, so if you make love to me again then I am not going to complain,” she murmured.

“When you mention being shot so casually it makes me crazy,” he told her stiffly. “I want to kill him for hurting you, Janice.”

“So I won’t mention it again.” She brushed the hair from his forehead. “You have to remember that I am still here David, and we have to focus on that.”

"I know," he said with a sigh. He rolled off her and to her surprise he picked her up gently.
"Where are we going?"

"I am going to give you a bath." He kissed her lingeringly on the lips. "A very long one."

*****

He finally relented and went to the office, insisting that she stayed at the manor where there were servants and his mother there to look out for her.

"You have changed his life," Julia commented, putting blackberry jam on the toast for her. She had come downstairs with David and he had kissed her lingeringly before he left, telling his mother to take care of his girl. "He told you about Eileen?"

"Not in a lot of words," Janice said with a smile. "You know David."

"Don't I," his mother said with a grimace. "A man of few words. We forced the marriage, his father and me and Eileen's parents. We were friends for a long time and we thought it would be a good match. He did not want to do it, but we convinced him that it would be okay and Eileen was already in love with him. Even the day before the wedding, he voiced the fact that he did not think it was a good idea because all he felt for her was a certain fondness like a brother would feel for his sister but I told him the love would come eventually. I was wrong." Julia sipped her coffee contemplatively. "He was never going to love her and it only made both of them miserable. He was too much of a gentleman to ask for a divorce, and if she had not died, he would have still be trapped into a loveless marriage and I tortured myself about that so many times." She reached out and touched Janice's arm. "You changed his life in a way that I never dreamed possible. I have never seen him so happy and I want to thank you for bringing him back."

"He has changed my life too," Janice said blinking away the tears. "I have never felt this way before and sometimes it is so overwhelming that I wonder if I can handle it."

"My love for his father was a comfortable one, nothing compared to what you two share." Julia nodded her thanks to a uniformed maid who set a bowl of fruits in the middle of the table. "Yours and David's is indeed something special and I am glad you found each other. Now to more pressing matters," she said with a bright smile. "We have a wedding to plan."

*****

"He seems to be quite a nice young man," Janet commented.

She and Richard were at home enjoying a quiet evening together. They had finished having dinner and were enjoying the fading light of the sun as they sat on the newly renovated porch wrapped up in a warm blanket.

"He seems to be very much in love with our daughter," Richard said thoughtfully. "I told him that I wanted to stay with her for a little bit when she was in the hospital, but he told me point blank that he was not leaving."

"He is a billionaire at that," Janet said in wonder. "I know of his company and that place has been in operation for a number of years."

"And he wants to marry her."

"Why wouldn't he?" she retorted. "She is an exceptionally beautiful girl."

“I am so happy for her,” Richard said with satisfaction. “I am so glad that you finally decided to take me back. I was devastated when I thought you would not.”

“I strongly doubt you were,” Janet said dryly.

“Do you have any idea how much I love you woman?” he asked her gruffly, turning her around to face him.

“I think I can guess,” she told him softly, reaching out to touch his cheek.

“I spent years thinking that I could manage life without you and for a minute I did until reality struck and I realized that it had to be you,” he mused. “We spent so many years together and I should have realized that spending so many years with a person meant that it would not be so easy to do without them.

“Remember the first time we met?” he asked her fondly.

“When you bumped into me at the farmer’s market?” she said with a laugh. “You knocked over my tomatoes and squashed two of the plumpest ones and insisted on buying me back a whole pound.”

“You looked at me as if you wanted to hurl the rest at my face,” he said with a grin.

“I almost did,” she said wryly. “And then you had the gall to invite me for coffee.”

“You turned me down flat,” Richard remembered. “And I saw you the next week at the same place waiting and you had tomatoes in a basket and how could I say no to that face?”

“It started right there,” he murmured. “I wanted to take you home then and there and ask you to marry me.”

“Why didn’t you?” She angled her head and looked at him.

“Because you were a terrifying woman,” he admitted ruefully. “And I was afraid you were going to turn me down.”

“I waited on you to ask me and I was starting to get frustrated,” Janet told him.

“You did huh?” He tilted her chin and looked at her familiar beautiful face, not quite getting why he had left in the first place. “You will never have to be again,” he said softly, bringing his head down for a kiss.

*****

Leah stepped inside the apartment tentatively as if she was expecting to see Lance pop out of a corner and confront her. It was the first time she had been back since the awful incident. She had been spending the time with Candace and her friend had insisted that she spent some more time there, but she had to get on with her life. Lance was locked up. He had regained consciousness and had asked to see her, but she had not gone to see him, she could not bear to see him after what he had done. The blood had been wiped clean, but she knew it was still there seeped into the floorboards, his blood as well as Janice's. She shuddered and dropped down on the sofa. One minute they were there chatting and laughing and the next minute they were facing the barrel of a gun that had almost taken their lives. He had been unhinged and she knew he would have killed them and killed himself. What makes a person go from being normal to becoming unstable like that, she thought sadly. He had reminded her of the happier times and in fact they had been happy in a tiny apartment, the newness of love surrounding them and the excitement of the plans filling their every conversation. They had made love every chance they got and had been eager to see each other when they got home from work. She remembered when they had had separate shifts and how mad they had been about the separation. They had gone to picnics and took strolls in the park when they were off and ate from each other's plates at the dinner table. It had started to go wrong a year into the marriage when he had seen her talking to a doctor and laughing with him. He had accused her of trying to trade him in for someone with a higher pay grade and even though she had tried to convince him that he was wrong, he had gotten progressively worse until she had stopped talking to people at work just so she could have peace of mind.

The last straw had been when he had grabbed her arm in public when she had waved to a guy she knew from some time ago. She had realized that there was no way that love was going to flourish in an environment like that and it was best that she walk away from it.

With a shudder, she buried her head in her hands and let the tears fall.

Chapter 12

Her parents were getting married in a private ceremony and a small dinner was going to be held at their home right after. It was November and the sky looked bleak and the trees stark.

Janice had gone back to the store and there had been a succession of weddings she had made floral arrangements for. She had been staying more at David's than at her house and she had told him that she was going to be sleeping at her own place tonight and he was welcomed to join her. It was Saturday afternoon and the ceremony was over within an hour and they left for the house.

Janice had gone there with Maggie and Jake to decorate the place. She had closed the store for the occasion and had placed her mother's favorite bluebells all around the living room where they were going to have dinner. It was set for three o'clock and her friends, David and his mother and Maggie and her husband and Jake and a few friends and neighbors were already there. Her arm was on the mend with just a little twinge of pain every now and then, but she tried not to mention it to David or he would not stop hovering. She adjusted the straps of her dark blue chiffon dress before going to adjust the floral arrangements on the table.

The guests were having pre-dinner drinks and David was talking to her father and several of the men.

She went towards Candace and Leah. “I thought you girls would be drinking,” she teased them when she noticed that they had nothing in their hands. Leah looked like she had lost weight and the dress she had on did not fit her very well.

“Do you think they made a mistake getting back together?” Leah asked her quietly.

“I don’t know about that honey,” Janice told her quietly, sensing the girl’s pain, her heat wrenching. “All I know is that they realized that they still love each other and they want to be together.”

“I tried to tell myself that maybe if I had given Lance a chance that he would not have gone off like that and maybe it would have worked,” she said despondently.

“I know you don’t believe that Leah,” Candace told her firmly before Janice could respond. “He had started getting physical and when that starts to happen then there is no turning back.”

“My husband whom I loved at one point is in prison for attempted murder,” she said in anguish, her eyes glistening with tears. “How do I come to terms with that? How do I accept that the love we had once shared is now turned into something so horrible?”

“Honey you have to stop torturing yourself with guilt and try to cope,” Janice told her softly. “I promise you that, Candace, and I will be there for you to get you through it.”

They both took her arms as the others turned to go into the dining area. Janice caught David’s eyes as he made to come over and he nodded perceptively and went ahead without her.

The dinner was lively and the conversation was ongoing. Janice stood up and made a toast.

“I want to say to my parents that I am so happy that they realized that they belonged together after all.” She gave a big smile in their direction. “I am happy to know that I will not be getting step parents after all.” There was a general laughter all around. “A friend of mine asked me how do you know if it is a good idea for two people to get back together and I think I know the answer to that. It is when you have been out there for a little bit and you realize that whoever you go out with after, they ended up coming up short and you cannot stop thinking about the person you thought you had gotten over. I recently discovered that feeling myself.” Her eyes swung to David who was seated beside her and their eyes met and held for a while. “When you have found the one and only who makes all others pale into insignificance then that’s how you know. Mom and Dad, I want to wish you all the best the second time around. I was not there for the first time so I am happy I am around to witness this one. Cheers.” She held her glass aloft and the others joined her with shouts of goodwill.

“Thanks, my love,” Richard Langley stood and held up his glass. “I thought it was over between Janet and I and I thought I could move on with someone else, but I was wrong and I thank goodness for second chances. To my wife, the second time around.” He pulled her up and kissed her lingeringly on the lips while the guests cheered.

David reached for her hand and held it underneath the table, not letting go until they were ready to eat, his touch snug on hers.

*****

That night while he was making love to her, he made a promise to her. “Whatever is happening with me, I promise to tell you. No secrets,” he whispered. He was still inside her and was breathing hard against her face.

“I promise the same and also if you leave me I will not be like Mom who allowed Dad to walk out of her life for five years. I will hunt you down and drag you back by your hair.” She sunk her fingers in his soft dark hair and pulled just a little bit.

“I believe it,” he said with a laugh, bending the capture her bottom lip into his mouth, nibbling on it and sending delicious tremors through her body.

He felt himself harden inside her and he started moving, gathering her hips as he pleasured her over and over again!

*****

“How about this one?”Candace asked her. They were looking at wedding dresses at the bridal boutique Julia had recommended. There were three weeks left for the wedding and the wedding planner was handling everything else, but Janice had wanted to pick out her own dress. It was a stunning off-white chiffon with a plunging neckline. The bodice was encrusted with glittering tear drop diamonds that sparkled and shimmered and the skirt fell in graceful folds all the way to the floor. “Go try it on.”

She did and when she turned to look in the mirror, her breath caught and held! It lit up her whole body and hugged her breasts to perfection. The flouncy skirt swirled around her and looked like a cloud gathered around her. She had lost a little bit of weight and it made her breasts looked even more generous. Her friends came in just then and let out squeals of delight. “Girl, this is it! This dress was definitely made for you,” Candace exclaimed.

Leah looked at her soberly and was brought abruptly back to her wedding day and how happy she had been then. With a determinedly bright smile she took Janice’s hands. “You look absolutely beautiful.”

"Thanks, honey." Janice looked at her searchingly. "Are you okay?"

"I am getting there," she said honestly. "I know that your marriage will turn out better than mine and that makes it very hard for me right now and I keep asking myself what I did wrong."

Janice pulled her outside the dressing room and they sat on the padded chairs available. "You fell in love and there is nothing wrong about that." She told her friend firmly. When she had told Candace that she wanted to go and look at dresses, she had wondered if it would have been too painful for Leah but the two girls were going to be her attendants so she had had to include Leah as well. "You are going to have to find a way of dealing with it and I know it is going to be difficult for you. How could it not be? But just know that Candace and I will always be there for you, it does not matter that I am going to be married, we are in this thing together, right Candace?" She looked over at her other friend.

"Friends for life," the girl said soberly, gripping Leah's hand closest to her.

"Thank you," she said tearfully. "Now let's get accessories."

*****

“She looked so woebegone, David,” Janice murmured sadly. They were curled up on the sofa half watching a romantic comedy on the television at her house. She had insisted they spent time at her place because very soon she would have to give it up and settle at his place and he had agreed. “I felt sorry for her.”

“Has she gone to see him?” Hs hands were loose around her waist and he planted a kiss on the top of her head.

“She does not want to. You think she should?” She turned her head to look up at him. He looked more relaxed these days and was smiling more.

“Maybe that is the only way she will get some closure,” he suggested.

“I will mention it to her.”

*****

The day dawned bleak with a tiny appearance of the sun peeking out of the heavy clouds. It had gotten decidedly cold. It was December 11th and the Sunday morning although cold and bleak showed the promise of a beautiful day filled with the blossoming of hope. The wedding was at one o'clock and her friends had spent the night at her place to help her get ready. She was served breakfast in bed by Candace and Leah made her bath.

"Are you nervous?" Leah asked her quietly as she handed her the large white fluffy towel to wrap around her as she climbed out of the steaming bath.

"To be joined with the man I love?"She shook her head. "Absolutely not. Are you sure you are okay?"

"I am," Leah said with a brief smile. She had finally been to see Lance and she had spoken to him. He had told her he was very sorry for what he had done and he should have gone and get help. She had left feeling a lot lighter. "I want you to enjoy this the most important day of your life and as much as we are friends, I don't want you thinking about me or anyone else than that delicious man you are getting married to."

"Thanks honey." She gave the girl a hug.

*****

He saw her coming up the aisle on her father's arm and he thought he was dreaming. She was beautiful! A vision that surpassed any other he had ever seen. The church was packed to capacity with family friends and employees of the huge operation that David was in charge of. He met her halfway and with a brief clasp of hand with her father he took her hand and placed it on his arm continuing up the aisle.

"Friends and family," the minister began as soon as the guests took their seats. "We are gathered here to witness the love between David Hattori and Janice Langley. If there is anyone here who objects to this union, let them speak now or forever hold their peace." He waited a spell before continuing. "A love between a man and a woman is something beautiful and pure and was ordained by God. The couple has requested to say their own vows so we will let them do so at this time. Please face each other."

"Janice," David said taking her hands in his. She had passed her bouquet to Candace. "I was drowning in guilt and defeat before I met you. I went through life with a mantle of grief on my shoulders, just existing and never living. You came into my life and I saw a ray of hope, sunshine bursting through the clouds and a brighter tomorrow and I never thought it possible.

You are so petite and yet you pack such a wallop! I love you, my darling, and will always love you no matter what happens or where we go, it will always be you. I promise to love, honor and provide for you and I also promise that I will always be there for you, in everything."

"David," she smiled through her tears. "I love you and I always will. You have shown me that in a world where love is sometimes superficial that it can be more than that and I promise to obey you, respect you and be your best friend from this day forward. I will be your wife and your lover and the person you turn to when you need a shoulder to cry on because I love you so much. With you I am not afraid to show you who I really am because I am not afraid to be open to you my love. I love you now and forever until the sting of death kisses our brows."

The silence was poignant in the small chapel and the two people who promised to love each other until death stood there staring at each other unaware of anyone else.

The minister cleared his throat and brought their attention back to him. "The rings please," he asked the best man.

David slid the double princess cut diamonds on her finger and she in turn put his on.

“By the power vested in me, I now pronounce you man and wife. You may kiss your bride, David,” he said with a smile.

He pulled her gently into his arms and his lips met hers slowly. She opened up for him and wrapped her arms around his neck, their tongues meeting each other in an explosion of emotions that had them clinging to each other.

“Ladies and gentlemen, I now present to you Mr. and Mrs. David Hattori,” the minister told them as they stood and cheered.

*****

The reception was held at the manor in the Great Hall. There was a fire blazing in the huge hearth. There were flowers everywhere and balloons suspended in midair with the colors they were wearing. Candace had worn a figure-hugging chiffon dress of rose pink and Leah had worn mint green. The dinner went off very well with various toasts to the newlyweds beginning with her father. “My wife insisted that I behave myself and do not say anything untoward,” Richard Langley said with a smile looking down at the very attractive woman dressed in soft peach on the chair beside him. “Janice is my only child and a more beautiful and loving and kind woman I have ever seen. She used to bring home every stray animal in the neighborhood because she could not bear to see them hungry or hurt and our house was always filled with one animal or another. When she was not tending to the animals, she was digging in the dirt and planting something or the other.” He laughed along with the rest of the guests.

“Dad!” she called out to him.

“Don’t worry honey, I will not let the guests or your new husband know how you cried over the plants when they died. Oops.” He laughed again as the guests burst into laughter. “Our daughter has been a source of joy in our lives and we are happy she has met a man who makes her so happy. Suffice it to say that if I hear one complaint from her I will forget how much I regard you David, and all bets will be off. Cheers to David and his lovely bride, my daughter.” He lifted his wine glass and the others with him.

*****

“How are you, Mrs. Hattori?” David asked her tenderly as they danced to the lovely instrumental the live band was playing on the raised dais.

“I am doing great, my husband.” She looked up at him and admired the way he looked in his ice blue jacket suit. “It sounds strange, and it is going to take some getting used to,” she murmured.

“I am already used to it,” he told her with an amused smile, his hands tightening around her waist. “When can we get out of here?”

“I suspect anytime soon,” she said with an impish smile. “Why the rush?”

He brought her closer to him and she felt it. “Need I say anymore?” he asked her huskily.

“No,” she whispered. “Let’s go make our goodbyes.”

But it was at that moment her father came over and he had to dance with her.

“So how is my little girl?” Richard Langley asked looking down into her exquisite face.

“I am happy and in love,” she said with a beaming smile. “And my parents are back together so what more do I need?”

“Probably to hurry up and give us grandchildren,” he suggested with a smile.

“Dad.” She gave him a warning look. “We are not quite ready yet. We are in the process of getting to know each other.”

“I know baby girl, your old man was just pulling your leg.” He kissed the top of her head. “I am glad you are happy.”

*****

They picked up the small bag they had packed and he took her on the private jet to the sunny state of Florida where they would be staying at private home owned by the company there. It was very secluded and came equipped with a swimming pool and a tennis court.

“No one lives here?” she asked wonderingly as he set her down inside the elegant living room. The furnishings were made from bamboo shoots and were a polished tan. There were rugs strewn all across the shiny wooden floor and gave the place a relaxed and homey look.

"We allow executives to stay here when they are in the Florida branch of the company," he told her. It had been a freezing ten degrees where they came from but it was a mild sixty degrees in Florida. "What would you like to do first?"

"I want to feel my husband's body on mine." She twined her arms around his neck.

"That can be arranged. I was planning to give you the grand tour but I guess later will do." He lifted her up and took her to one of the large bedrooms.

"This is beautiful," she breathed as he put her on the bed. The wall was painted in a blush pink and the furnishing was white with pink shells all around them.

"You are beautiful," he murmured coming beside her on the bed. "I saw you walking up the aisle and my breath stopped and I could not breathe." She had changed into a simple blue and white dress that tied at the neck. He pulled the string and his intense dark eyes took in her unfettered breasts, the nipples already hardened. "I can't believe you are my wife." He bent his head and sucked her nipple inside his mouth, pulling on it so hard that she felt the pull straight down to her pubic area. She dug her fingers through his soft dark hair, her body arched against his. He lifted his head and looked at her. The pins had fallen out of her curls and her black hair was spread over the soft white sheets making a startling contrast. He pulled down her dress and took off his clothes hurriedly, coming back on the bed with his painfully stiff penis in his hand, pulling back the foreskin, his eyes on hers. She reached out to touch the tip of him, her nail grazing the opening and causing him to shudder. She rubbed at the moisture there and then put the finger into her mouth and sucked on it. He watched her, his penis hardening even more and he knew he had to have her right now. He lifted her legs and placed them on his shoulders, inserting his erection inside her. She moved against him, her bottom grinding against him as he thrust inside her forcefully. He removed her legs from his shoulders and opened them wider to gain more access to her, his thrusts becoming more urgent and demanding. Janice gripped the sheets tightly as she felt him deep inside her, his erection touching her core and sending shudders through her entire body. He pulled out of her suddenly and started rubbing the tip of his penis on her mound, his eyes narrowed as he looked at her flushed face. “Tell me you want me,” he said tightly, holding his erection in his hand and touching her briefly.

“I want you,” she cried, her body consumed by the desire he had awoken inside her.

He pulled her up to him and entered her and as she wrapped her legs around his waist he thrust inside her, whispering in her ear and causing the shiver to ignite the already open flames licking at her!

Chapter 13

"So how was the honeymoon?" Maggie asked her as soon as she reached into the store the Monday after she came back. She had a wedding on Wednesday and she wanted to make the arrangements herself. David had taken her shopping and had bought her so many clothes that she wondered when she was going to get the chance to wear them. "We have dinner parties all the time for out of town associates so you will get a chance to wear them. And besides I love to spoil you," he had whispered into her ear.

They had stayed naked for most of the time and he had taken her out to fancy restaurants and shown her the sights. They had even gone to Disneyworld.

"It was too magnificent for me to tell you in details," Janice said with a beatific smile as she placed her pocket book inside the office. Christmas was fast approaching and she had a pageant to make some arrangements for. It was going to be a Christmas unlike any others because she was going to be spending it with her husband at the manor and there was going to be a company dinner that was going to be hosted by them and by them it meant she and his mother would make the arrangements. She was wearing one of her new outfits, a black wool dress pants and a pink and white cashmere sweater. Her hair was caught up in a ponytail and diamonds winked at her lobes, a gift from her husband on their last day on their honeymoon.

"You don't have to give details because girl you look like a billion dollars," Maggie said with a grin. "Oh wait! That's how much you are worth!"

"Cut it out, Maggie," Janice warned with a smile. "What have we got for today?"

*****

She got home before he did. He had also given her a car, the one she had been admiring in the showroom that day some time ago. He was always giving her things and she had tried to stop him but he would not hear of it.

"Hi Julia," she greeted her mother-in-law who was on her way to the dining area.

"Hi dear, how are you?" The woman beamed at her. They had come back from their honeymoon to see some changes in his suite. She had had the dark furnishings removed and replaced them with neutral colors and the sheets had been changed as well. Janice had been surprised to see that her clothes had been sorted and put inside the huge closet that held her husband's clothes. Julia was glad that they had no intention of leaving, she was enjoying the company.

"I am starving," she admitted with a laugh, shrugging out of her white cashmere coat and blinking as a maid materialized out of nowhere and came and took it from her. "I still cannot get used to that," she admitted ruefully.

"You will after a while." Julia linked her arm through hers and guided her towards the dining area. "Will David be joining us for dinner?"

Before Janice could answer, they heard a noise in the hallway and realized that he had come home. "Speak of the angel," Julia said with a smile.

"Hi Mother." He greeted her with a kiss on the cheek before pulling his wife into his arms and kissing her soundly on the lips.

"I thought you had a late meeting," Janice protested.

“I rescheduled it for tomorrow morning. I looked outside and noticed that it was snowing and I wanted to come home and suggest we go play in the snow,” he told her with a grin.

“You want to go play in the snow?” It was his mother who asked the question, a look of amazement on her face. She had never seen him like this before. He looked animated and as eager as a boy.

“Yes I do.” He looked down at his wife. “What do you say?” he asked her softly.

“I would love to.” She kissed him gently. “Race you to the suite.” With that, she pulled out of his arms and raced towards the stairs. Julia watched as her son ran after her, his laughter echoing inside the house. Out of the corner of her eyes, she saw the household help coming out one by one and looking after them in amazement. Janice had done wonders to her son and for that she would be forever grateful!

*****

They bundled up and went outside. It was just flurries, but they did not mind and David watched as his wife stuck out her tongue and caught the snowflakes daring him to do the same.

He loved watching her and the way she was so energetic and fun and totally unaware of how truly beautiful she was. “Okay, how about something to eat?” she asked, launching herself into his arms. “Your poor wife is starving.”

“And we cannot have that, can we?” He pulled her closer to him and kissed her cold lips. “Let’s go and get something to eat.”

*****

Later that night, he told her about living with Eileen. He had never spoken to her in details about it before and she waited until he was ready to share with her.

“I knew from the beginning that it was not going to work,” he said soberly. She was curled into his arms and her head resting against his chest.

“You are sure you want to talk about it?” She lifted her head to look at him.

“I want us to be able to talk about anything no matter how we feel about it.” He looked at her, his dark eyes intense. “I want to share the bad things and the good things.” His hand cupped her cheek tenderly. She nodded and slid back down to rest her head on his chest. “At first, I thought that because we were friends that maybe we could make it work eventually and over time I could come to love her. I hardly ever made love to her because it was more of a duty than anything else.” His hands tightened around her body and she could feel his regret. “I was not a man who was used to a lot of women because I hated that and when I realized that I had to force myself to be with her then I started to feel resentment towards her.”

She lifted her head to look at him and his dark eyes met hers. “You cannot force love David, and she knew what she was getting into when she agreed to marry you,” she told him quietly. “I hate that both of you suffered so much, but there is nothing you can do about it now.”

“I know,” he told her softly. “I love you, Janice, so much that my body is filled with it and I shudder to think that I would have gone through life with something so commonplace as living with someone I did not love. The feelings you evoke inside me is so unbelievable wonderful that I cannot contain myself. I have no regrets right now believe me.”

“I am happy to hear that.” She lifted her head and slide on top of him. “I am not going to resent a woman who had no place in your heart and even if she did, I would not have resented her either. I love you David, and that is all that matters right now.” She bent her head and took her lips with his tenderly. He shuddered against her and let his hands drifted down to her bottom. She reached between them and eased up a little bit to put his penis inside her, closing around him. “I am done talking.” She whispered as she lifted her body and started to ride him, grinding down on his as he thrust up and into her. “David,” she moaned and swung her legs over on the bed sitting up and gasping as his penis went straight up inside her. He held her hips firm and eased off the bed to thrust inside her forcefully, his eyes holding hers, his body trembling with passion!

*****

“We don’t get to see you anymore,” Leah complained. They were having a girls’ night at the manor. David had tactfully left and took his mother out to dinner to let them have their time together. It was Saturday night and Janice had invited them over to hang out and spend the night as well. The chef had prepared a variety of snacks and finger foods and the wine was chilling in the cooler. They were in the hall with the fire blazing in the hearth and Janice had spread a blanket for them to sit near the fire. “That's not true,” Janice told her firmly reaching for a bacon wrapped potato. “You saw me last week when you wanted me to follow you to pick out a dress to wear to some nurses' function or the other.” She had no idea what to eat, everything looked so delicious. There were also Antipasti pizza, fried mozzarella, upside down mushroom tartlets, and mini Asian crab cakes.

“That was a brief moment and you were hurrying e along because you had to get back to the store to arrange some flowers for delivery,” Leah said.

“And I have not seen you in two weeks,” Candace spoke up.

“Now that one is your fault,” Janice told her. “I called you and you told me you were up to your ears in meetings.”

“That's true.” Candace sighed. “That place will kill you with meetings.” She chose the fried mozzarella and crunched on it in appreciation. “Is the chef single?”

“He is happily married,” Janice told her with a laugh.

“How on earth you stay slim with cooking like this?” Leah asked her as she ate the upside down mushroom tartlets.

“David has a kick-ass gym somewhere downstairs and we are not afraid to use it,” she said, leaning back against the mound of pillows behind her.

“Look at you married to a billionaire and it is actually a love match and the man is actually very handsome,” Leah said with a laugh. She looked more relaxed these days and laughed more which was a relief to her friends.

“I cannot believe it myself,” Janice mused.

They chatted about this and that and then they went down to the room with the gym equipment and had a hilarious time trying out the different ones. They drank the whole bottle of Chardonnay, and David and his mother came home and saw them curled up on the blanket fast asleep. His eyes zeroed in on his wife who was spread out on her stomach with her hand thrown over her head.

“Are you leaving her there?” his mother whispered.

"I do not sleep without her," he said simply, making his way silently to where she was, careful not to wake her friends.

She smiled and nodded. It was the answer she had expected.

He lifted her up gently and she opened her eyes to look at him. "David?" she murmured. "I am not drunk, the wine just made me a little sleepy." She snuggled closer to him.

"I should hope not," he whispered. "Let's get you to bed."

She waved languidly at her mother-in-law and rested her head back on her husband's muscular chest, totally contented.

*****

He undressed her gently and put on her nightgown before pulling the comforter over her. She stirred slightly and reached up to pull his head down to hers. "I love you," she murmured, kissing him softly and then she drifted off to sleep. He stood there looking down at her, his expression unbelievably tender.

*****

Being married to Richard again was different the second time around. He was more thoughtful and considerate, and he would take home flowers and chocolate for her for no apparent reason. They went out on dates, something they had scarcely done in the past and they did things together.

It was getting closer to Christmas and they were planning on having a small dinner party which had to be done either on Christmas Eve or the day after Christmas because they were aware that their daughter and her husband were planning a huge party at their place.

“How about a turkey?” Richard suggested lazily. They were in the living room drinking hot chocolate and warming themselves by the fire.

“You know I don’t like turkey,” Janet said with a shake of her head. “I was thinking more of roasted chicken, ham, and pot roast beef and some salads to go with it. Maud makes the most scrumptious pumpkin pie this side of the country so she promised to make some for us.”

“So it’s settled then.” He pulled her legs towards him and slide off her fluffy bedroom slippers and started kneading the in sole of her feet.

"That feels so good," she murmured, leaning back against the cushions in the sofa. "We actually look like old married people," she added with a grin.

"Far from it," he said mildly, pulling her into his arms. "Very far from it," he whispered against her lips as he went in for the kiss.

*****

Leah sipped her latte slowly, determined to enjoy the very last sip. She had been on her feet from the morning and she had slipped out to the coffee shop to just relax and breathe something else aside from antiseptic and alcohol and people running around trying to save lives. She looked up suddenly and saw him looking at her. He stopped looking as soon as her eyes met his. She had seen him in here before and noticed him looking at her, but she had not given him any encouragement. She was not ready for dating much more a relationship because the incident with Lance had shaken her up so badly that she just wanted to spend time by herself. He looked like he was some sort of an executive in a business suit and he was tall and well built with close shaven hair. His skin was the color of melted chocolate and he looked damn good! Too bad she was not interested. She was getting up to leave when he approached her.

“I have been trying to work up the courage to approach you.” His very white teeth flashed into a smile and her breath caught. He was handsome! “My name is Jason Ramsay.” He held out a hand and with a slight hesitation she took it briefly.

“Leah Whyte.”

“I was going to ask you if I could buy you another cup of latte, but it appears you are leaving,” he said with a smile.

“Look, Jason Ramsay,” she said, determined to set him straight right then. “I was married and it turned disastrous and almost ended up in him murdering me and my friends, so I am not looking for a relationship at this point.”

Instead of backing away, he stood there looking at her. “I am sorry you and your friends had to go through that,” he told her quietly. “But I promise you that I will never love you to the point where I think about hurting you.”

It was Leah's turn to stare. He was very serious and she felt a smile lifting the corners of her mouth. "I have to go, my lunch time is up."

"Here's my card, call me anytime you need a friend to talk to." He handed her the card. She looked at it and realized he was an investment banker.

"I already have friends," she told him.

"I am willing to be another one," he told her in a hopeful voice.

"We will see," she said with a small smile. "Nice to meet you, Jason Ramsay."

"The pleasure is all mine, Leah," he murmured. She walked out aware that he was watching her walk away and for the first time in a long time she felt a spring in her steps!

*****

The decorations were in place. She had closed the store yesterday afternoon after making sure the orders had all gone out. She had decorated the tree with him, dragging him into doing it after he had protested he had no idea how. Her friends had come over and were spending the night again and they were having a tree decorating party. There was food on the side table and Christmas carols were playing softly coming from the hidden speakers placed strategically in the ceiling. There was fire blazing in the hearth and the conversation was lively.

“We need a ladder for the star,” Julia said as she looked at the towering pine tree with its beautiful lights and decorations hanging onto it.

“I have a better idea,” Janice said mischievously. “Crouch down darling,” she told her husband.

“What are you up to, Janice?” he asked her.

The others started to laugh as they realized what she was going to do.

“You’ll see,” she told him, jumping on his back. As soon as he straightened, she went on his neck and he held her firm as she reached up to place the star on top of the tree. “There.” The others clapped and cheered. “Okay, you may let me down now,” she told him.

He shook his head and reaching up he plucked her from his neck and held her in his arms refusing to let her down. In front of her friends and his mother, he took her inside the doorway and underneath the mistletoe and stood there with her in his arms. “We need to christen it,” he told her huskily.

“I agree,” she murmured, sliding her arms around his neck. He took her lips with his and just for a moment they forgot that they had an audience. When they broke apart, they realized they were alone in the large room.

“We cleared the room,” he murmured.

“Good,” she whispered, bringing his head back down to hers.

*****

The party was a success! She wore one of the many gowns he had bought her; a shimmering ruby red which clung to her shapely curves and highlighted her generous breasts. He had given her rubies for her Christmas among the many gifts and the earrings sparkled at her lobes and the stone settled just between her cleavage. Her hair was wrapped in a severe chignon on top of her head and showed off her delicate ears and her sculpted cheekbones. She looked stunning and David could not take his eyes off her. She walked the room and mingled with the guests. Her parents were also there and they looked so happy together that Janice felt her heart almost bursting with joy. “Mom, you look like a star,” she murmured hugging the older woman.

“And you look like one of those rich society women we so often see in magazines. Baby, you look stunning,” Janet told her proudly.

“Thanks, Mom.”

“Apart from your mother, you are the most beautiful woman in this room,” her father told her drawing her in for a hug.

“Dad, you have to say that,” Janice told him with a grin.

“I mean it, just ask this young man here.” She turned around as her husband slid his hands around her from behind.

“Ask me what?” He nuzzled her neck.

“That she is the most beautiful woman in the room aside from her mother of course,” Richard said with a grin.

“I am afraid I don’t agree,” he murmured softly looking down at his wife. “My wife is the most beautiful woman on the planet. No offense, Janet,” he told his mother in law.

“None taken darling,” Janet told him with a fond smile.

“Are you guys having fun?” David asked them.

“You really know how to throw a party,” Richard commented.

“All due to my lovely wife,” he murmured.

“Don’t forget that Julia helped too,” Janice reminded him.

“You did most of the work,” he murmured, tipping her chin and placing a lingering kiss on her lips. He heard his name being called across the room. “Duty calls,” he said lightly. “Would you please excuse us?” he asked her parents politely.

“Of course,” Richard told him.

“I will talk to you later, Mom and Dad.” With a wave, she was gone with her husband’s arm around her waist.

“That young man is totally besotted with our daughter,” Richard murmured, staring after them.

"As it should be," Janet said with a sigh. "How about dancing with your wife?"

The party went on until the early hours of the next morning with the guests leaving one by one. They were finally able to go up to their suite but before they went to bed he held her to him and peeled off the exquisite dress from her supple body, his hands touching every inch of her, his mouth following suit.

Chapter 14

Leah saw him again at the coffee shop. She had to admit that she had been looking forward to seeing him. She had not called him, had only kept looking at his card over and over again. At one point she had thought about getting rid of it, but she had decided against it; after all, it was just a card. She had not told her friends about him because she knew what they would say. So she had kept it to herself.

It was the day after New Year's Day and she was on the early shift so she had come out to get her usual latte and as she was sipping the hot liquid she saw him come in. Her heartbeat quickened when he came in. He was wearing black dress pants, light pink shirt, and black and grey sweater with a pink and black tie. His eyes zeroed in on her as if he had been expecting to see her and he walked over to her.

"I have been waiting on your call," he told her with a smile.

"I have been busy," she said with a shrug. To her consternation he sat in front of her. She wished she had put on a little makeup but working as a nurse in a hospital was not designed for putting on artifice. Her hair was piled on top of her head and secured by a jeweled clip and she was wearing a dark blue sweater underneath her light blue scrubs.

“You are going to tell me that being a nurse you don’t have time for yourself,” he said in amusement. “But what are you on now? The morning shift? So how about dinner later after you have gone home and gotten some rest? Come on, help a brother out here. I have been thinking about you since I don’t know when and I want to get the chance to know you better if you will let me. I assure you I am not a stalker. I have a mother and a father who are very proud of me and two sisters who think the world of me. I do not have a baby mama or two living somewhere with a string of kids and I make a very good living. Oh, and I live on my own in a very nice apartment.”

“That’s quite a bit of information.” Leah could not help but laugh.

“See, I managed to do that,” he said softly, reaching for her hands. “I want the chance to be able to do that more often, please.”

Leah stared at him, feeling the warmth of his touch on her. “Okay,” she nodded. “Here is my card.” She handed it to him. “You may call me later and we can decide where to go.”

“Good.” He looked down at the card and looked back at her. “I will call you later.” He stood up as she got up from her seat. “And Leah, I do not give up easily and I am not going anywhere,” he told her quietly.

She stood there looking at him for a spell and then went on her way, a smile curving her lips.

*****

Janice was making the plans. It was David’s birthday on the 9th of January and he was turning twenty-eight. His mother had told her that he did not like the fuss of birthday parties, but she was going to change that. It was going to be a Saturday, and she was planning to get him out of the house on the pretext of taking him out to dinner and then she was going to take him back to the house where the real party was going to be.

“Are you sure this is a good idea?” Julia asked her uncertainly. They were in her suite where she was working on some tea mugs she had orders for and Janice had the list in front of her. Today was Tuesday, and she was planning a huge party for the weekend and everything was not in place yet.

"About what?" She looked up at her mother-in-law in surprise. She had just come home from the store and had just taken off her boots and was curled up on the sofa in Julia's sitting room ready to discuss the party with her.

"About the party?"

"Of course I am sure," she said a little impatiently. "My husband is not going to be mad at me for throwing him a party, he is in love with me."

"Obviously," her mother in law said in amusement, looking at the exquisitely beautiful girl who had changed her son's life for the better. She had heard David laughing so often that she had to wonder if it was the same man who had been so taciturn and unapproachable several months ago. "He hates surprises, Janice."

"He is going to love this one," Janice said firmly. "There are going to be balloons, a clown, bounce about-" She broke off as she saw Julia's shocked expression. "I am just pulling your legs, Julia, relax," she said with a laugh.

"You had me going there for a while," Julia said, her hand on her chest. "Okay, what do you have so far?"

*****

She sounded him out when he came home that evening. He had been coming home earlier since they had gotten married and only when he had late meetings that he left the office a little late and he tried not to schedule meetings past office hours.

She was propped up on some pillows and was reading a book when he came inside the bedroom. They usually had dinner with his mother, but sometimes they ate in their suite. He jumped on the bed and put his head in her lap. “How is my wife?” he asked her softly.

“Your wife was here wondering when you were coming home,” she told him, putting aside the book and kissing him soundly on the mouth. “It’s seven-thirty, David,” she complained.

“I know baby, but the meeting ran over and I was chafing with impatience. A new shipment came in today and we had to strategize a plan to get them out of the various showrooms. We have a massive ad campaign to formulate and the sales team needed a pep talk.”

“So, all of that made my husband late in coming home to his eagerly waiting wife.” She pulled his tie open and started unbuttoning his shirt. “Have you eaten?”

“Pierre fed us, but if you were waiting to eat with me, I can eat something again,” he said swiftly.

“I ate with your mother.” She had finished unbuttoning his shirt revealing his white undershirt. “How about after you take a shower, we open up a bottle of wine and sit by the fire and just relax?”

“Sounds good.” He kissed her lingeringly on the mouth and then hopped off the bead to go to the bathroom.

*****

“So Saturday is your birthday.” She swirled the red liquid in her glass and watched as the flames played against it. He had showered and come out with only a towel wrapped loosely around his narrow waist and his hair was still damp. “What do you want to do?”

“Just have a quiet dinner with you.” She was between his open legs and was leaning back against him. “That’s enough.”

“So no excitement and opening of presents?” She asked looking up at him.

“You are the only gift I need.” He kissed the tip of her nose.

“Ah, that’s so sweet.” She grinned at him. “If by any chance you are saying that to make me feel obligated to tell you the same thing in June when it’s my birthday, think again buddy,” she warned him.

“I would never expect that from you,” he told her in amusement. “I expect you will want the whole works: party, presents, clothes, money, possibly a new car and should I go on?” He lifted one heavy brow at her.

“I will make a list,” she said smugly. “What’s the sense of being married to a billionaire if I don’t get all of those?”

“No sense at all.”

She had set aside her wine glass and turned to face him, shrugging off her thin robe revealing her nakedness. “All this talk about birthdays and gifts has gotten me horny. How about you?”

“Same here, but you don’t need to say anything to get me hot and on fire for you,” he told her huskily, resting back as she pulled the loose knot of his towel. He was already hard and ready for her. She dipped her fingers into the bottom of the wine glass and wiped them over the tip of his penis.

“Jan,” he whispered.

“It’s a pre-birthday gift,” she told him huskily, rubbing her fingers all over him.

“I love it,” he said in a strangled voice as she bent her head to lick him off. “I love it very much!”

*****

“Will there be strippers?” Candace asked her. They were having lunch at the nearby restaurant where they had ordered beef stew to combat the freezing weather.

“The only stripper my husband needs to see is me,” Janice told her mildly.

“I totally agree with you,” Leah said with a laugh.

“What’s with you?” Janice asked her curiously. She had noticed that the girl was laughing more now and she looked happier.

“What do you mean?” she asked, bending her head to sip her stew.

“Yes, I noticed how happier you look these days,” Candace commented. “Oh Lord, give us peace! You met a man!”

“So because I happen to look more relaxed and contented it has to be a man?” Leah asked in exasperation.

“Not necessarily, but unless you tell us that you have received salvation then it is definitely a man,” Candace retorted. “So which is it?”

“Okay fine, I met someone!” she said, throwing up her hands in defeat.

“You met someone and we had to drag it out of you?” Janice asked her with a frown.

“I did not want to say anything yet because I was not sure,” Leah protested.

“So you are sure now?” Candace asked.

“We had dinner on Tuesday,” Leah said a smile bursting from her. “It was absolutely wonderful,” she said her eyes sparkling. “He is an investment banker and he is single and is very close to his family: his parents who have been married for thirty-five years and his two sisters: one is a lawyer and the other is a psychiatrist.”

Her friends stared at her in amazement. “You really like him,” Candace said slowly.

“He liked me first,” she said defensively. She told them how he had been checking her out for sometime at the coffee shop near the hospital and had worked up the courage to hand his card to her and invited her out.

“Did he kiss you?” Candace demanded.

“What?” Leah looked at her friend askance.

“Did your lips meet his, Leah?” she continued impatiently.

“We kissed when he dropped me off,” she admitted reluctantly. “It was unbelievably amazing!” she said in a rush.

"I have never felt that way before and I had to fight not to ask him to come in."

"Girl you are in trouble," Candace murmured.

"Why do you say that?"

"Don't listen to her." Janice cast her friend a dry look. "I think that's wonderful, honey."

"You don't think it's too soon?" she asked anxiously.

"Of course not!" Candace said sharply. "After what that creep put you through, you deserve a break."

"I still love him Candace," Leah said soberly.

"Of course you do, honey." Janice gave Candace an exasperated look. "He was your first, but that does not mean there is not room for someone else. I can't wait to meet him."

"I was planning on asking him to David's birthday party, do you mind?"

"Of course not! I think that's wonderful."

"We are happy for you, honey," Candace said soberly, reaching for her hands. "You deserve it."

*****

"Would you zip me up?" Janet turned her back to her husband for him to pull up her zipper. They were getting ready for David's party which was slated to officially begin at nine p.m.

"I would much prefer to zip you down," Richard murmured, sliding the rich burgundy dress off her shoulders and placing several lingering kisses on her shoulder blades.

"Richard Langley, you need to stop at once, we cannot be late," Janet warned him, her heartbeat quickening.

"We are not going to be late," he murmured, sliding the dress further off her. He was already in his dress pants and his blue striped cotton shirt was open. "Just a little sugar for your husband."

"I can't believe you just said that," Janet tried to sound stern but she failed miserably as he cupped her generous breasts in his big palms, his fingers rubbing the nipples.

“Give your husband something to sustain him through the night.” He stepped around to face her and slide the bra from her shoulders. “I need to suckle.” He bent his head and pulled a nipple inside his mouth causing her to sag against him boneless.

*****

“Where are we going?” David asked her as she dusted the foundation on her smooth cheeks. She was already dressed in a stunning black slinky dress that molded her figure and left nothing to the imagination. It came up high to her neck and plunged all the way down to the top of her bottom, making her not able to wear a stitch of underwear. Her hair was piled on top of her head and secured ruthlessly with pins and diamonds sparkled at her lobes and on her wrists. David wanted to ask her to take off the dress and wear something less seductive but he did not want to appear to be a jealous possessive husband.

“To the new restaurant opened a few blocks away called Memories.” She took up her black clutch and turned to face him. She was unbelievably beautiful and sexy.

“Will we be staying long?” He wanted to tear the dress off her and plunged inside her. And the fact that she was not wearing any underwear was making it worse.

“Why? Do you have somewhere to be?” She was staring up at him mischievously.

“Yes, inside you,” he growled.

Janice felt her breath caught and held at the look on his face. “In that case my totally insatiable husband, the sooner we get there the sooner we can leave.” They had made love in the early hours of the morning when she had woke him up with her lips on his body and her hand pumping his penis, and they had spent the most of the morning in bed making love. She had insisted he stay in bed and had gone down to the kitchen to supervise his breakfast and had it brought up and had joined him in bed where they had eaten the wheat toast, blueberry pancakes with whipped cream and strawberries, coffee and orange juice, and a small cupcake.

After that, they had taken a shower together and that had turned into them exploring each other’s bodies and then they had gone downstairs where his mother had handed him a ceramic cup with their wedding pictures on it.

*****

The restaurant was far from crowded and they were seated in a corner booth where they placed their order. “Happy birthday darling, I hope that you will have many more of these and I will always be there to celebrate with you,” she murmured, lifting her glass of champagne to his.

He clinked his glass to hers and noticed that she was attracting the eyes of most of the men in the room. “Remind me next time to lock you up in our suite and throw away the keys,” he told her dryly.

“Whatever for?” she asked him her eyes twinkling.

“Jan, every male eyes in this room are looking at you,” he told her stiffly. “Couldn’t you have worn something less revealing?”

“Baby, this is not revealing, and you were the one who bought this, remember?” she asked him.

“I did not!” he retorted.

“You ordered a batch of clothes for me and this was one of them,” she reminded him, trying not to laugh at his expression.

"You are not wearing it again, unless we are going to be alone," he told her darkly. "I am going to fire that personal shopper."

"You are not," she told him firmly. "She has good taste." She leaned forward and took his lips with hers, nibbling on his bottom lip. "You are going to have fun taking it off me later," she told him softly.

"Janice," he groaned. Her tinkling laugh rang out bringing more attention to them as the men stared at her exquisite face.

*****

"I am glad we are out of there," he said with relief as he negotiated the car through traffic on their way home. It had started to snow and the white droplets clung to every surface, giving it a faint ghostly appearance. "Even the Maitre D who brought your coat was staring at you."

"You sound paranoid," she told him mildly.

"I am not," he muttered. He had been in a constant state of arousal all through the dinner and it was only the thought of entering her when they reached home was comforting him. "It's good to be home," he said with a sigh as he drove the car around the circular driveway. She had instructed the guests to park in the neighboring lot and some of them were parked all the way around. It was a good thing that the grounds were so massive.

He had wanted to go around to the back, but she had insisted they walked at the main door. "Why is it so dark?" he wondered as he opened the door.

Shouts of happy birthday had him stepping back and his eyes narrowed as the lights came on and he noticed the amount of people with wine glasses in their hands. "Janice," he murmured in an undertone, turning to look at her, seeing the plans of ravishing her disappearing through the window.

"Happy birthday, darling." She closed her hands around his neck. "Be nice, we went through a lot to pull this off," she whispered in his ear.

"I will deal with you later," he warned her.

“Looking forward to it,” she told him, blowing in his ear causing the desire to spiral inside him. She was definitely going to pay big!

*****

It was a lively party with a live band playing the music and the food was exceptional. The chef including Pierre from the office had done a terrific job. The cake was a towering red velvet with his picture on the top and they all gathered to sing happy birthday to him. He kept her firmly beside him, his hand closing around hers as if he was afraid she would be taken away from him.

She met James and had to admit that he was everything Leah said he was and to her amusement she saw how he could not take his eyes off her friend.

She greeted her parents and had a laugh with Julia about how surprised David was and mingled with the rest of the guests, most of them from his office. Maggie and her family were there and also Jake along with a date. Candace had come with a guy she had met a week ago. The meal was buffet style and people heaped their plates with the delicious food.

It was a little bit later that the three girls had a chance to talk.

“So what do you think?” Leah asked her friends anxiously as they stood in one corner of the massive room sipping champagne. Janice glanced over to where her husband was talking to some of his board members. He looked up just then and their eyes met and held, causing a shiver to run up her spine.

“I think he is a keeper,” Janice told her dragging her eyes away from her husband.

“I agree, he is gorgeous girl,” Candace told her.

“Good,” Leah said with a sigh, looking over to where James was talking to several of the males at the party. He looked up and saw her and excusing himself he headed over.

“Have fun,” Janice told her going back to her husband.

It was after twelve when the party broke up and they waited until every guest had drove off exclaiming how much fun they had had.

*****

“So did you have fun?” Janice asked him as soon as they were in their bedroom. He had taken off his jacket and his tie and had unbuttoned his shirt.

“I did,” he told her with a smile. “But you are still required to pay for your subterfuge.”

“I fully expect to be punish,” she murmured, slipping out of her dress. She stood before him completely naked apart from the mile high black heels she had on. “So I am waiting for my spanking.” She walked over to the bed raised on the dais. And bent over on the bed, her legs parted.

He never ever dreamed that he could get more turned on by her, but he was so wrong. He almost destroyed his clothes in his hurry to get them off and he could feel his heart trembling inside his chest as he hurried up the steps to get to her. “You are going to kill me,” he told her hoarsely. He entered her without finesse, he did not have the time or patience to do otherwise, and holding her hips firm he thrust inside her, his movements frantic and needy. He could feel the heaviness inside his testicles and knew he did not have long before he spilled inside her. She bucked against him, her hands clenching the sheets as she gave him as good as she got!

www.SaucyRomanceBooks.com/RomanceBooks

*****

Later that night, much later as he held her to him, their shuddering at a minimum he told her thanks. “For what?” she asked him huskily, raising her head to look at him.

“For turning my grief into a love that is so alive and strong that it has transformed my life,” he said shakily.

“You are most welcome my husband,” she told him softly, wiping away tears from his cheeks. She snuggled close to him and closed her eyes in contentment, never dreaming there could be such happiness!

The end.

If you enjoyed this ebook and want me to keep writing more, please leave a review of it on the store where you bought it. By doing so you'll allow me more time to write these books for you as they'll get more exposure. So thank you. :)

Get Free Romance eBooks!

Hi there. As a special thank you for buying this book, for a limited time I want to send you some great ebooks completely

free of charge directly to your email! You can get it by going to this page:

www.saucyromancebooks.com/physical

You can see a the cover of these books on the next page:

www.SaucyRomanceBooks.com/RomanceBooks

www.SaucyRomanceBooks.com/RomanceBooks

These ebooks are so exclusive you can't even buy them. When you download them I'll also send you updates when new books like this are available.

Again, that link is:

www.saucyromancebooks.com/physical

Now, if you enjoyed the book you just read, please leave a positive review of it where you bought it (e.g. Amazon). It'll help get it out there a lot more and mean I can continue writing these books for you. So thank you. :)

More Books By Mary Peart And Friends

If you enjoyed that, you'll love When He Comes Back Around by Mary Peart (sample and description of what it's about below - search 'When He Comes Back Around by Mary Peart' on Amazon to get it now).

Description:

When Jewel and Jordan were 15, they were high school sweethearts.

Jewel was certain she had met the boy of her dreams, until he unexpectedly moved away to Europe and left her broken-hearted.

Fast forward into adulthood, and Jewel is happily content with how her life is going.

That is, until she discovers Jordan has returned to take over his father's business, and is looking to reconnect with the love of his life.

Jewel wants this too, she really does.

But time changes things, and despite being as dashing as ever, Jordan has a lot of making up to do.

Will the two be able to reconnect lost love after all these years?

Or will Jewel be left broken-hearted for a second time, with even worse consequences?

Want to read more? Then search 'When He Comes Back Around Mary Peart' on Amazon to get it now.

Also available: Her Asian Billionaire's Perfect Match by Mary Peart (search 'Her Asian Billionaire's Perfect Match Mary Peart' on Amazon to get it now).

Description:

Leonie doesn't really believe in love.

Which is funny, considering she runs a match making service for over 50s, and her entire job is based on finding love for her clients.

But her beliefs are about to be called into question.

One day a potential client enters Leonie's office accompanied by her son.

John Masaki is a billionaire who wants to make sure of the service's legitimacy before signing his mother up.

Upon meeting Leonie however, he soon becomes convinced he's found his own match in her.

Will the loveless Leonie be able to overcome her beliefs and pursue something she never thought she'd want?

Want to read more? Then search 'Her Asian Billionaire's Perfect Match Mary Peart' on Amazon to get it now.

You can also see other related books by myself and other top romance authors at:

www.saucyromancebooks.com/romancebooks

CPSIA information can be obtained at www.ICGtesting.com
Printed in the USA
LVOW10s1430010716

494932LV00016B/666/P